THE SECRET ENEMY

It is the height of the Cold War. British Agent Steve Carradine's mission is to locate and smuggle to the West a defecting Russian scientist with the vital secret of a new technology — but the Soviets are hot on his trail. Aided by a mysterious female agent, Carradine finds Professor Ubyenkov, and the three fugitives make a desperate flight on the Orient Express in a superhuman effort to remain alive and escape to Britain.

Books by Manning K. Robertson
in the Linford Mystery Library:

SEEK AND DESTROY

Warwickshire County Council

06/14			
Ken			

This item is to be returned or renewed before the latest date above. It may be borrowed for a further period if not in demand. **To renew your books:**

- **Phone the 24/7 Renewal Line 01926 499273 or**
- **Visit www.warwickshire.gov.uk/libraries**

Discover • Imagine • Learn • *with libraries*

Warwickshire County Council

Working for Warwickshire

SPECIAL MESSAGE TO READERS

THE ULVERSCROFT FOUNDATION
(registered UK charity number 264873)
was established in 1972 to provide funds for
research, diagnosis and treatment of eye diseases.
Examples of major projects funded by
the Ulverscroft Foundation are:-

- The Children's Eye Unit at Moorfields Eye Hospital, London
- The Ulverscroft Children's Eye Unit at Great Ormond Street Hospital for Sick Children
- Funding research into eye diseases and treatment at the Department of Ophthalmology, University of Leicester
- The Ulverscroft Vision Research Group, Institute of Child Health
- Twin operating theatres at the Western Ophthalmic Hospital, London
- The Chair of Ophthalmology at the Royal Australian College of Ophthalmologists

You can help further the work of the Foundation
by making a donation or leaving a legacy.
Every contribution is gratefully received. If you
would like to help support the Foundation or
require further information, please contact:

THE ULVERSCROFT FOUNDATION
The Green, Bradgate Road, Anstey
Leicester LE7 7FU, England
Tel: (0116) 236 4325
website: www.foundation.ulverscroft.com

MANNING K. ROBERTSON

THE SECRET ENEMY

Complete and Unabridged

LINFORD
Leicester

First published in Great Britain

First Linford Edition
published 2014

A catalogue record for this book is available
from the British Library.

ISBN 978–1–4448–1942–7

Published by
F. A. Thorpe (Publishing)
Anstey, Leicestershire

Set by Words & Graphics Ltd.
Anstey, Leicestershire
Printed and bound in Great Britain by
T. J. International Ltd., Padstow, Cornwall

This book is printed on acid-free paper

1

OPENING GAMBIT

The crescent-shaped, sandy cove flanked by huge rocks and pine trees glowed brilliantly in the light of the setting sun and the stiff breeze blowing onshore had whipped up the waves that came rolling in on the beach from somewhere far out near the horizon. Inshore, the white-sailed fishing boats bobbed slowly up and down at anchor as the tide came moving in on a surging swell. Leaning his shoulders back against the small breakwater, Steve Carradine thrust his legs out straight in front of him, feeling the smooth, dry sand working its way between his toes. He let his gaze wander idly over the whitewashed houses of Tamariu. He had chosen this spot deliberately. It was, even now, sufficiently unspoiled and away from the main tourist routes for his liking; yet there were

1

wooded mountains close at hand and he had spent much of his time skin diving among the coral beds just offshore, spearing fish.

The sun was getting lower, but the air still held that deep, balmy warmth which he had now come to associate with this part of the Spanish coast. There were few other people on the curved expanse of beach. Two healthy-looking men, their skins tanned to a deep brown, which showed they were natives of the place, were seated on the deck of one of the fishing boats less than a quarter of a mile out in the bay. Further along the beach, in the direction of the small hotel, set among the trees which, at that point, almost reached to the water's edge, three girls came up out of the sea, ran towards the breakwater, their arms and legs throwing a cascade of sun-glittering drops onto the sand as they snatched up their towels, drying themselves vigorously. Carradine let his glance slide over them, stiffened a little as a sudden, brief flash of sunlight, reflected off glass caught his attention. It came again a few seconds

2

later, enabling him to pick out its position quite clearly. The window of the room immediately above his own, sunlight reflecting off the lenses of powerful binoculars. He peered more closely at the sun balcony just outside the window, but could see nothing. Whoever was up there, watching the beach, evidently did not intend to be seen from below and only the chance gleam of sunlight on the glasses had given his presence away.

He turned his attention away from it and got slowly to his feet, feeling the soft touch of the sea breeze on his body. The three girls had run up the beach, along the white pathway, which led around towards the hotel. Now, apart from himself and the two men on the boat, the place seemed to be utterly deserted.

The air was still warm, the sun still sufficiently high for one last dive in the sparkling clear water just off the rocky stretch of coast where the coral beds glowed a rich, warm pink beneath the deep blue of the ocean. As he walked slowly towards the water, he donned his gear, checked the spear-gun, then climbed out on to the out-jutting rock which overlooked the deep pool, the multi-filamentous coral just visible several feet below the surface. He dropped feet-first into the water and dived through the upper layers where the slanting rays of the sun still managed to penetrate, then further down into the deep blue depths. It was a breath-taking panorama down here in the utter silence of the ocean bed, a heart-catching beauty such as he had known nowhere else in the world.

Pink blended with blue and indigo violet at this depth and he swam lazily over the stretching coral beds, the spear-gun nestling lightly in his hands. Multicoloured fish darted in profusion over the bottom of the ocean, gliding in and out of the coral strands, scattering as he swam close to them, vanishing into the blue distance, then reappearing with an almost startling rapidity. He idled below the surface for the best part of fifteen minutes without taking a shot at any of the denizens of the sea-bed, then decided that the feel of the water was becoming cold on his body, took a snap aim at a silver fish which glided between two rising pillars of pink some twenty feet away, saw with a faint sense of chagrin the spear miss by at least a couple of feet. In a way though, he was glad that he had not scored a hit; it would have been —

His thoughts gelled abruptly in his mind as something sleek and brilliant shot past the edge of his vision, just glimpsed out of the corner of the goggles he wore. There was an uneasy tensing of the muscles of his stomach as he recognised the object before it disappeared into the dimness. Another slim metal spear fired from a weapon similar to that which he carried.

Squirming swiftly, instinctively, he threw a quick glance over his shoulder and caught a glimpse of the dark shape swimming swiftly away among the coral. A split second later, the would-be killer had vanished. He thrust himself cleanly through the water, sliding a spear into the gun, cocking the weapon, ready to fire. Reaching the spot where his assailant had vanished, he glanced curiously about him.

The other, whoever it was, had swum deliberately out to sea, moving into deeper water. Reluctantly, Carradine moved back in the direction of the beach. By now, the man would be among the fleet of fishing boats and it would be like looking for a needle in a haystack trying to find him.

He bobbed his head above the surface as he came up from the deep blue depths, looked about him. The two men he had noticed earlier were still lazing on the deck of the boat riding up and down at anchor. One glance was sufficient to tell him that neither of them had been the silent attacker. Nothing moved among the other boats. Pausing for only a moment, he pulled himself out of the water and stood on the rock as he pulled off his diving gear. He rubbed the back of his hand over his eyes where the rims of the goggles had bitten into the flesh. There was a feeling in his mind at that moment which was so familiar now that it had almost become a part of himself; the feeling of danger all about him. It was something he had to come here to get away from, if only for a brief period.

Smiling wryly, he picked up his gear and walked slowly in the direction of the hotel. It seemed that danger and he were inseparable, that the more he tried to get away from it, the more it followed him. Unconsciously, almost, the sun was touching the skyline now where the blue ocean blended almost imperceptibly with the sky, and there was a slight chill in the breeze. Climbing the whitewashed steps swiftly, he made his way inside the building. The thought flicked through his mind that perhaps now might be a good time to try to discover the identity of that quiet, watchful observer who had been taking such a studied interest in what was going on along the beach. It was just possible that whoever it had been, may have seen something out there, which could give him a clue as to the identity of that underwater assassin who had tried to kill him. He quickened his step as he passed through the doorway of the hotel and made his way towards the desk in the long, spacious lobby.

The receptionist looked up and gave an

oily, ingratiating smile: 'Ah, Señor Carradine. You enjoyed your swim in the bay?'

Carradine gave a slight nod, took the key to his room from the other, and held it in his hand for a moment. 'The room immediately above mine,' he said. 'Can you tell me who occupies it?'

The other smiled wetly. 'Of course, señor.' He ran a forefinger down the page of the register. The smile widened appreciably. 'I think I understand. That is Señorita Francesca Romano's room.'

Carradine gave him a cold smile. 'Somehow, I don't think you understand at all,' he said, turning on his heel. He made his way up to his own room and turned the key in the lock. The tiled floor near the window was warm under his bare feet and the filmy curtains billowed into the room, flapping against the side of the half-open window. He glanced out onto the sun terrace below. There were a few brown bodies stretched out in the inclined deckchairs, sunglasses still covering their eyes, although the sun had gone down and the sky had lost its harsh, glaring appearance. The smell of flowers and suntan lotion drifted up to him and he wrinkled his nose for a moment, then moved away from the window and stepped into the shower. He doused himself with cold water, the fine needle sprays stinging his flesh, icy-cold but invigorating. Towelling himself dry, he dressed, glanced at his watch and saw that it was almost nine o'clock.

Dinner was served at nine-thirty and acting on impulse, he left his suite and wandered up the winding stairway. He had reconnoitred the hotel on the day of his arrival, knew every corner, every turn, in the building. Two minutes later, he was standing outside the room directly above his own. What could he say when he knocked on the door and confronted the girl who occupied this room? He couldn't very well come right out and say: *I noticed you watching me with high-powered binoculars and I was wondering if you noticed anyone in a skin-diving outfit shortly after I dived in, because whoever it was tried to kill me.* There had to be a more subtle approach than that.

If the girl spent her late afternoon and

early evenings spying on people on the beach, then the chances were that she had a very good reason for doing so, that it was something more than mere curiosity. Francesca Romano. He turned the name over in his mind for a moment, but the file he kept in his brain failed to come up with anything; he had never heard the name before.

He knocked and there was a long pause before the door opened. Carradine's first view of Francesca Romano was startling. She was tall, the deep blue-violet eyes almost on a level with his own. She had pale blonde hair that swept down to her shoulders, framing a perfect oval face, the skin lightly sunburned, mouth warm and generous, although now there was a sense of suspicion about the way her lips were pressed together, and her brows were arched in a mute question.

She said in a low, smoky voice: 'Yes, what do you want?'

There was a faint trace of accent to her voice that Carradine did not recognise — Eastern European probably.

'My name is Carradine, and I'd like the

answers to a few questions,' he said lightly. He inclined his head towards the interior of the room. 'I'm sure we can talk more informally inside.'

For a second, the girl hesitated and he felt certain there was a faint gleam of fear in her dark eyes, a look which she tried to force away as she stood on one side to allow him to enter. Going inside, he threw a quick glance through the window and saw that from there, as he had guessed, it would be possible to see the entire sweeping curve of the beach and the fishing vessels out in the bay; and with binoculars one could see a lot more besides.

'I'm afraid I don't know why you're here or how I can help you.' She stood with her back against the wall near the door, letting her gaze wander over him, brows still raised appraisingly.

Carradine smiled at her. 'It's very simple really.' Going over to the window, he said softly: 'You've got an excellent view of the bay from here, even better than I have, just below. I should think you could see everything that goes on out there.' Turning, he walked over to her, took out the slender cigarette case and held it out to her. She took one, bent forward as he flicked his lighter, and sucked the smoke into her lungs, the movement emphasising the line of the high cheek bones.

'That was the reason I took this particular room.'

'I see. And also why you brought along a pair of binoculars?' He saw her start, saw her face immediately tense.

'Binoculars? But why should I — ?'

Carradine shrugged and slipped the lighter back into his pocket. He saw that she was concentrating on trying to find an answer to him, that she was instantly on the defensive. Her eyes probed him, wondering how much he knew and why he was there; what all this meant to him.

'It's quite immaterial to me why you should be so interested in what is going on out there,' he said quietly. 'But maybe you ought to realise that when the sun is setting, there's a good chance of sunlight reflecting through the lenses. That's how I spotted you late this afternoon. I was hoping you might be able to tell me something.'

'If I can.' Still on the defensive, she now watched him with a strangely curious stare.

'No doubt you saw me skin-diving about half an hour ago. Did you see anyone else go into the water shortly after I did?'

Was there a faint flicker of something at the back of her eyes as she studied him more closely? He was unable to make up his mind. It was, he thought, as if she had, just for a second, lifted a veil from them and allowed him to see all the way down into her mind and then, equally swiftly, the veil had been drawn back over them and they were almost as expression-less as before.

'You were alone on the beach when I saw you,' she said flatly. 'There was no one else around while you were underwa-ter.'

'The two men on the nearest fishing boat — you saw them?'

'Oh yes, but they were there all the

time. I assure you that neither of them left the boat.'

'That's what I thought.' He nodded and sucked deeply on the cigarette.

'Why are you so interested in what happened while you were diving?'

Carradine smiled. He closed his fingers around her arm. 'It's a long story and I'm not sure whether you'd believe it. Suppose you let me tell you about it over dinner?'

For a moment, he thought she was going to refuse, then she nodded her head very slightly. 'Very well.' Her lips parted in a smile. 'Who knows, it may prove to be a very interesting and entertaining evening.'

★   ★   ★

She was seated at the table looking out on to the terrace when he entered the long dining room, her chin in her hand, eyes focused on the far reaches of the sea, for it had now assumed a deep blue colour, matching her eyes.

'I've already ordered,' she said as he sat

14

down. 'I hope you don't mind.'

'Not at all.'

Two vodka martinis arrived, each with a thin slice of lemon peel in them. Carradine sipped his appreciatively, watching the other guests moving into the room to take their places. He recognised several of them; the three girls he had noticed on the beach that afternoon had a table to themselves in one corner and were talking among themselves in low voices, occasionally throwing glancing looks in his direction.

'I always find that the vodka here is the nearest to that of Russia I've ever tasted,' said the girl after a brief pause, during which she eyed him with a faintly amused glance over the rim of her glass.

He lifted his brows slightly at that. 'I wouldn't have said you were Russian,' he observed.

'I'm not.' She smiled now, probing him with her eyes. 'My mother was Romanian and my father English, but I was in Russia for five years just after the war. Foreign correspondent on a London newspaper.'

'What happened?'

Francesca looked down into her drink for a long moment, turning the glass between her fingers. 'How do you know that anything happened?' she asked.

Carradine shrugged. 'I suppose it's just natural to assume that something did. Several friends of mine have worked behind the Iron Curtain, but after a few years they had to return home. I got the impression that the Reds disliked anyone working there for too long. At the end of a few years one can generally become reasonably fluent in the language and it's conceivable that one can pick up something they would have preferred not to become known.'

Francesca smiled grimly. 'You're right, of course. It was nothing definite. Just a series of little incidents designed to make my life more difficult. Finally I got so mad at the game — I didn't show it, of course — that I just wired my paper and asked to be allowed to return to London. I think they must have understood, because five days later I was back in England. I suppose you could say I was running away, but it isn't easy for anyone who hasn't been there to know how they run things when they want to be rid of someone.'

Carradine felt amused at the change in the girl. He had already decided that she was well able to take care of herself in any situation. Now it was obvious that she had plenty of experience. 'I know exactly what you mean,' he said, setting down his empty glass on the table.

The look in the girl's eyes said that she had suspected he might, that she had guessed he was a little different from the usual run of tourists who came to Spain.

Two waiters came and hovered over them as the main meal was served: shellfish and a sauce made of melted butter and spices in a lavish boat. They ate in silence and Carradine was forced to admit that the girl had taste when it came to choosing the food served there. Champagne followed, bubbling and sparkling as it poured from the slender bottle, the ice forming a pale mist on the glass.

Finishing his second glass, Carradine

sat back in his chair, nodding his head appreciatively. 'That was an excellent meal,' he agreed. 'I admire your flawless taste, Francesca.'

'Thank you. And now, may I ask how I can help you? I gather you did not ask me to have dinner with you just to talk of Russia and the work I did.'

Proffering his cigarette case, Carradine waited while the girl had taken one, lit it for her, then drew deeply on his own and said quietly: 'I know this may sound strange, possibly hard to believe, but someone attempted to kill me while I was diving this afternoon. The beach was deserted when I went in for the last time, and I guess I was submerged for about a quarter of an hour when someone took a snap shot at me with a spear-gun. Fortunately their aim was somewhat worse than mine normally is; even so, it was a near thing. I'm hoping I can find out who it is that wants me out of the way so drastically.'

'And you're hoping that I saw someone on the beach after you went into the water?'

'That's the idea. You must have seen me go in.'

She hesitated, then nodded. 'I did. But there was no one else, I assure you.'

Carradine looked the girl in the eye. 'You're sure about that?' It seemed almost impossible to him that anyone could have slipped into the water anywhere along the beach and not have been seen by someone with binoculars at that window above his. Either the girl was lying for some reason, or there was something he had overlooked.

'I'm quite sure.' There was no doubting the sincerity in her tone. 'Did you see anything at all of the man who attacked you?'

'Very little, I'm afraid. It was dark down there on the seabed and when he saw that he had missed with his first shot he didn't wait to try a second, but turned and swung out towards the deeper water.'

'Then doesn't that suggest he was heading for one of the fishing boats out in the bay?'

'It's possible. And you saw nothing on any of the boats?'

'No.' A pause and then: 'Why should a person want to kill you, Mr. Carradine? I mean, there's no reason, is there?' There was something artless in her look, which did not fool Carradine for a second.

'In my line of work, there is always a reason why someone would want to kill me,' he said, his voice grave, sincere. 'I've had to kill men in my time and I suppose that by the law of averages, there are those who have been ordered to kill me. It could be that — ' He broke off suddenly as one of the waiters approached the table. The other coughed discreetly.

'There is a telephone call for you, Señor Carradine. You may take it in the corner booth.' The other merely inclined his head in the direction of the three small telephone compartments set side by side at the far end of the room.

Carradine rose slowly to his feet. 'If you'll excuse me for a moment, Francesca,' he said the girl. 'Even on holiday one can never get away from it all.'

'You make it sound like trouble,' murmured the girl softly. There was a curious look in her eyes. Then she glanced away, her gaze sliding in the direction of the door, and the expression changed a little. For a moment, once again, Carradine was certain he saw fear reflected at the back of her eyes. Swiftly, as he moved around the edge of the table, he turned his head. The man who had just entered the dining room was short, fat, rapidly balding, his head glistening a little in the light, forehead faintly beaded with perspiration. A man who disliked heat, Carradine thought. The small eyes were wide and staring, looking around the room as though searching for someone known to be present. For a second, they rested on Carradine's face, then moved on with a somewhat bored expression, treating him as someone of no consequence. It was a look of a man who did not care whether Carradine was dead or alive; his presence there had been noted, but that was all.

For a moment, he felt a faint stir of anger, then dismissed it at once. He gave the girl one final look, then followed the waiter across the room into the booth, closing the door behind him.

Lifting the receiver, he waited for a moment while the high-pitched humming on the line ceased. Then there was a sudden click and a harsh, metallic voice asked: 'Is that Mr. Stephen Carradine?' The accent was distinctly noticeable, magnified by the faint hum.

'Speaking.'

'You won't know who I am, Mr. Carradine,' purred the voice. 'I merely wish to give you a friendly piece of advice. The climate in Tamariu can become very uncomfortable at this time of the year.'

'That sounds like a warning — or a threat — to me,' Carradine said tightly. 'I don't like threats.'

'Mr. Carradine,' continued the voice inexorably, without the slightest inflection. 'Your inquisitiveness can make things very difficult for yourself. And also, I may add, for your very charming companion. Curiosity, as you may both discover if you persist in it, can have troublesome, if not fatal, consequences.'

'That's very clearly put,' Carradine said.

The other ignored the interruption. 'There is a coach leaving Tamariu at eight o'clock precisely tomorrow morning. I trust you will see reason to be on it.' The sharp click told Carradine that the other had replaced the receiver. For a moment, he stared down at the black receiver in his right hand as if trying to force it to tell him more than he now knew. Whose was that voice which had warned him off in no uncertain terms? What had he been on the point of discovering here in this tiny village with its quiet, peaceful bay and whitewashed houses? It seemed incredible that anything could be happening here; yet now he came to think of it, it was in such places as this, out-of-the-way, old-worldly places, where he seemed to stumble on the most trouble.

Vaguely, he wondered whether it was something they ought to know about in London, and whether he ought to get a call through to them. After a little heart-searching, he decided against it. Whoever it was, these people obviously considered that, as yet, he knew so little of it that they could afford to let him leave the place on that early coach in the morning. Unless, he reflected grimly, they had already made other plans for him, intending to rid themselves of him permanently somewhere away from Tamariu, where there could be no awkward questions asked concerning his disappearance.

Stepping out of the booth, he made his way back to the table and paused as he realised that the girl was no longer there. Wrinkling his brow, he glanced out on to the terrace. Possibly she had gone outside; the air was still warm and this was undeniably the best part of the day. He went outside. There was a couple standing against the rail a few yards away, but apart from them, the terrace was deserted. Puzzled, he went back into the main dining room and paused near the table. There was no scribbled note to explain why she had suddenly left like that, without any warning.

And what about this girl; this beautiful woman who had obviously been frightened of that man who had entered the room just as he was leaving to take that telephone call? What in hell was she supposed to be doing? Spying on someone on the beach? If so — why? What did she have at stake that made her so interested in what was going on at this place? That warning he had received had also mentioned her.

Making his way over to the door, he buttonholed the waiter standing just inside the room. The man was helpful and showed no surprise at Carradine's question.

'Certainly, señor. Señorita Romano left a few minutes ago. She seemed to be in quite a hurry.'

'Was there anyone with her when she left? A short, stout man for instance?'

The other shook his head. 'No, señor. She was quite alone.' There was a falseness to the other's tone that made Carradine think twice about asking his next question. If money was not enough to make this fellow say the right things at the right time, there was little doubt that other pressure could be brought to bear on him.

Yes, Carradine thought, as he walked

into the lobby and moved across to the desk, that's how it would be — a discreet word here and a couple of hundred pesetas there and anything could be hushed up. He leaned forward over the desk and shook the dozing clerk by the shoulder. The other stirred and jerked himself awake.

'You would like your key?' He pulled himself to his feet, stretched out an arm towards the rack behind him, and paused with his hand in mid-air, fingers brushing the keys.

'No, just a little information.'

'Information, señor?' The clerk gave an oily smile. 'You are looking for somewhere to go this evening? Tamariu is not a large village, but in the main street there is — '

'I'm looking for Señorita Romano. We were having dinner together, but she left in quite a hurry. Has she gone up to her room?'

'I haven't seen her. And her key is — ' The other shifted his glance, then nodded. 'Still here,' he finished.

Carradine's eyes were thoughtful as he

nodded and stepped back from the desk. Taking his key, he made his way quickly to his room, pulled the small travelling case from its place under the wardrobe, opened it, and took out the Luger pistol which nestled snugly in one corner. Sliding a fresh clip into place, he slipped the weapon into his pocket and went out again, locking the door behind him. There was that feeling in his mind again, a sensation which he had learned over the past years never to ignore.

The narrow winding alley that led down to the waterfront was quite deserted when he entered it and on both sides, the shadows were long and dark. He walked swiftly through an area of high-walled, terraced gardens, passed beside a small church, then almost at once he was moving down to where the fishermen had laid out their nets over the low stone wall that looked down on to the bay. He had a vague impression of the street gleaming a little in the last glow of sunset; then he was making his way up an arched lane, coming out on to the flat stretch of ground which angled out towards a gentle, sweeping curve of the bay itself, the water glistening faintly where it stretched out to the darkened, almost invisible horizon.

There was a flight of steps, innocent of any protective handrail, leading down on to the sand. At the bottom, he paused to look about him, straining his eyes and ears for any slight movement or sound. It was then that he heard it, faint but unmistakable. The pop-pop of an engine starting up. In the instant of hearing it, Carradine debated whether to run forward and throw caution to the wind in the hope of getting down to the beach before the boat pulled away, or whether to be careful and move slowly. It was just possible that there was someone left behind to watch the area.

As he made his way over the upthrusting rocks that littered this section of the beach, he heard the sudden roar of the engine gathering volume. Seconds later, he saw the boat, still tied to one of the small landing stages less than two hundred yards along the beach. In the faint light, he made out the trio of figures close behind it: the slender figure of Francesca Romano between two more burly figures, one on either side of her.

Two things impressed themselves on his brain in that same instant. One was that the girl was not leaving of her own accord. The other was that the short, rotund figure standing near the prow of the boat was the man he had seen entering the dining room at the hotel just before he had gone to the telephone. Inwardly, he cursed himself for his own stupidity. A blind man would have been able to see that the call had been timed fortuitously, as it had been no coincidence it had been made at that precise moment. Everything had been done to take him off balance, to get him out of the way while the girl had been abducted from the hotel and brought out here.

What could he make of it all? Was this a kidnapping? A prelude to murder? The voice over the phone had warned that the girl had been too inquisitive for her own safety. Somehow, he told himself fiercely, he would have to try to stick close to her, at least until he was able to prove to himself that his own deadly conclusions about what was happening were wrong.

Moving away from the shadows, his fingers resting lightly on the assuring metal of the Luger in his pocket, he padded over the sand. At any moment, he expected one of the men to turn and see him, to raise the warning; and when that happened, he knew he would have to move fast if the girl's life was not to be put into immediate danger.

But the danger, when it did come, came from none of the small group clustered around the boat at the small wooden jetty. The figure that moved forward out of the shadows was close by and moved silently. Carradine caught a glimpse of the upraised arm and saw the flash of light on the knife blade that plunged downward with a vicious speed, aimed at his chest. It was all over in five seconds — literally. Stepping to one side, completely on balance, Carradine struck the other's down-plunging arm just above the elbow with his own and shifted his left hand around the other's wrist, stopping the knife-point in mid-air with the tip less than two inches from his chest. There was a sudden sharp bleat of agony from the other, and the ominous cracking of wrist bones as Carradine twisted his left hand sharply.

The man swung, tried to jerk Carradine sideways, and sucked air in through his tightly-clenched teeth as the movement merely served to jerk his own arm back in a vicious hammer-lock. The knife dropped from suddenly nerveless fingers as Carradine forced the arm up between the man's shoulder blades. As a judo hold it would probably have been frowned upon by a purist; as a defensive move it was highly effective. The other's knees buckled with the pain that lanced along his arm. He tried to turn his head, mouth opening to yell a warning to his companions at the boat. Before he could utter a single sound, Carradine's hand, stiffened into a vicious weapon of destruction, caught him over the Adam's apple. His body went limp, slumping noiselessly onto the sand.

There was no more danger from him. Carradine let out a long breath, half-sigh, half-whistle. Within fifteen seconds, he was forcing himself over the rocks, running towards the jetty, but already he was too late. The powerful motorboat was already a couple of hundred yards out from the shore, thrashing through the water, creaming foam behind it as a churning propeller thrust it forward at an ever-increasing speed. In the bows, he could just make out the shape of the girl, the wind whipping her hair back from her forehead. It was useless to try to pursue them. Carradine knew that instinctively. There was not a boat in sight apart from a broken-down rowing boat a few yards away, which was in such a dilapidated condition that he doubted if any competent authority would ever give it a certificate of seaworthiness. For a long moment, he stood there in the deepening dusk, feeling the cool sea breeze on his face which congealed the perspiration on his forehead and along the muscles of his back, as he stared out into the dimness which had spread itself like a dark, velvet cloth over the sea. The motor-boat had almost vanished now; it was just visible at the end of the curving wake that stretched out behind it. A couple of seconds later, it swept out of sight behind the cluster of fishing boats standing off in the small harbour.

With a conscious effort of will, Carradine retraced his steps to the point where he had left the unconscious assassin. At least, he told himself grimly, this man would talk — and he would tell the truth. Whatever was going on here, he meant to know of it before the night was through. Where they had taken the girl. What they intended to do with her. Why they had threatened him and made two attempts on his life. He was used to danger. In his profession it was something he was forced to live with. The British Secret Service was no place for babes or those with a squeamish disposition. But he liked to know why he was being made the target of would-be assassins.

Picking his way forward through the rocks, he approached the place where the unconscious man had slumped to the ground when he had delivered that judo chop to his throat. The ground was empty!

Going down on one knee, he let his sensitive fingertips move over the sand. A moment later, he found what he was looking for, what he had half-suspected. The furrow in the sand where a body had been dragged soundlessly towards the stone pathway leading up towards the village.

2

A WIDENING WEB

The three-quarter moon burned along the sky off to the right of the plane, glinting brilliantly through the square window next to Carradine's seat. The faint, eardrum-vibrating whine of the jet's engines were just audible inside the pressurised cabin, almost on the edge of hearing — a background noise that, in spite of its faintness, still managed to grate slightly on his nerves, setting his teeth on edge. He forced himself to relax, tilting the inclining seat so that he was lying almost supine. Slowly, he let his gaze wander over the faces of the other passengers, those who were visible to him from that position.

They looked to be the ordinary run-of-the-mill tourists one usually met on the night flight from Madrid to London, most of them asleep or giving the appearance of sleeping. He closed his eyes, tried to pull his thoughts into some kind of order. Inwardly, he felt a little angry, dejected and frustrated. That message which had arrived for him that morning, delivered to his room by one of the waiters. Why would the Chief want him back in London so urgently that he had made him break his holiday and, above all, why had the fates decreed that it should arrive at that very moment? Now it seemed as though he were running away from Tamariu because of that telephone warning and he still did not know what had happened to Francesca Romano. There was a suspicion at the back of his mind that she had been removed to prevent her from talking, that she had perhaps discovered something of importance to those people. When the message ordering him to take the evening plane had arrived, he had been on the point of refusing it. Several ideas had flashed through his mind as he had read it. He could get the people at the hotel to say that he was no longer staying there, that he had left and given no forwarding address. No, that had been dismissed as soon as it had occurred to him. In his position, he had to leave word where he could be found; that went without saying. So what else had been left to him? To deliberately ignore it, and face the music once he did get back to London? To get in touch with Headquarters and inform them of what had happened, hoping maybe that permission would be given to him to stay on and get to the bottom of the whole mess? In the end, he had realised that there was absolutely nothing he could do. He had made the necessary arrangements, had caught the plane, and now here he was, flying at eighteen thousand feet, with most of the other passengers asleep around him and only the quiet, unobtrusive movements of the stewardess as she walked occasionally up and down the central aisle.

Settling his shoulders back in his seat, he let his thoughts drift idly. What could be on the Chief's mind now? he wondered. Another mission in some remote corner of the world? It seemed more than likely. Whenever one of the Government departments came up against something that involved a foreign country they had to call the Secret Service and one of the agents would be sent to deal with it. He closed his eyes wearily. Why couldn't one of the others have been briefed for this job? Why did they have to drag him back all the way from Spain? The other agents he knew were all good men. They had to be; the Chief had picked them himself, and knew them intimately. Carradine had read one or two of their dossiers himself when he had been put on normal duty at the London Headquarters between spells abroad — exhaustive dossiers which had given everything. He smiled a little to himself as he reflected how much the Reds would give to get their hands on those secret documents. Thank God they hadn't or things would be even more difficult and dangerous than they were at the moment.

The stewardess stopped beside his seat and looked down at him with a faint expression of concern on her face. 'Can I get you anything, sir?'

'If you've got anything that can blot out memories — yes; if not, then there's nothing anyone can do for me.' He smiled a little and saw her brows crease slightly.

'Sorry, I suppose I shouldn't be talking like this. I'm all right, really. Just finding it hard to get to sleep. Maybe a straight bourbon if you have one.'

'Certainly, sir.' She gave him another sideways look, then hurriedly went back to the rear of the plane. The jet whined on, high above the clouds, which were clearly visible as a great sea of billowy cotton-wool, gleaming like opalescent pearl in the bright moonlight which flooded down on them. When the bourbon came, he sipped it slowly, savouring the touch of it on his tongue and the back of his throat. The stewardess had stood beside his seat for a few moments longer than were absolutely necessary, clearly concerned about him, but not wanting to show it, then she had returned to her place and the long passenger cabin was quiet and undisturbed.

Carradine gave a deep sigh, rubbed his shoulders against the back of the seat, holding the glass in his right hand, watching the amber liquid swirl around it as the plane banked to starboard. He saw the great white mass of moonlit cloud tilt up towards him, then slip away as they straightened out on course again. What lay below that vast mass he did not know.

Finishing his drink, he set the empty glass on the small tray beside him. Perhaps he would be able to get some sleep now, he thought. Stretching his legs out straight in front of him, he closed his eyes, hands resting in his lap. The muted whine of the engines acted as a soporific and the faint swaying motion of the plane was a strangely pleasant sensation.

* * *

All the lights were on the whole length of the plane when he woke. He stood and fought his way up from the depths of exhausted sleep. Painfully, he eased himself back up from his inclined position until he was sitting straight. A quick glance out of the window confirmed that it was still night, but there was no sign of the moon in his field of view and if anything the cloud layer seemed closer now. Then he was fully awake, tired, his heavy eyes focusing automatically on the luminous dial of his watch. Five-thirty. He had been asleep a little more than an hour and a half. No wonder he still felt dog-tired.

'Coffee, sir?' The stewardess stood beside him, a tray with several cups of steaming coffee in her hands.

'Thank you.' Carradine struggled upright and rubbed the muscles at the nape of his neck with his left hand while reaching for one of the coffees with his right. 'Where are we now?'

'We'll be arriving in London in fifteen minutes. There was a storm over northern France and we had to make a diversion around it.'

Carradine nodded. The cup burned his fingers and the coffee was hot and strong, but it shocked some of the life and feeling back into his body and he sipped luxuriously, sighing in contentment. The note of the engines changed. The plane had dropped lower through the misty cloud and for several moments it was impossible to make out anything through the window. Over the pilot's door a red light flashed into being and beneath it the instruction to fasten his safety belt and extinguish any cigarette he might be smoking.

A quarter of an hour later, the plane touched down. There was a faint bleat of tortured rubber from the wheels, then their speed was slackening appreciably as they neared the end of the runway, turning on to the wider concrete of the perimeter track, taxiing around towards the control buildings.

Inside the building, he moved through the passport check into customs, and waited for his luggage to come off the plane. He was cleared with the minimum of fuss and delay and at the entrance to the airport found a car waiting for him. The chauffeur, a tall, quiet man, placed his luggage in the boot, then slid behind the wheel.

In the greying light of an early dawn,

the streets looked oddly depressing. There was a faint sheen on them, which told him it had been raining through the night and in spite of himself, he shivered. If there was anything he hated, it was London during or just after rain.

The driver was one of the Chief's men, silent and taciturn it was true, but a man who might know a little as to why he had been recalled with all of this vital urgency.

'Are we driving straight to Headquarters?' he asked, lighting a cigarette and letting the smoke trickle in twin streams through his nostrils.

'Those were my orders,' replied the other. He hesitated. 'However, if you wish to — '

'No, go ahead. I've no doubt the Chief has something pretty important on his mind to interrupt my holiday just as things were getting interesting in Spain. But seriously, have you any idea what he wants in such a goddamned hurry?'

'All I know is that you're to check with him as soon as we get there.'

Carradine turned his head and stared at the other in disbelief for a moment, then let his breath go in a long, muted whistle through his teeth. 'Hell, it must be important for the Chief to be there at this hour, waiting for me.'

That was quite true, he reflected, as he leaned back and watched the tall, grey buildings, all curiously stereotyped in a strange grey anonymity in the early morning light. There had been many occasions, he himself knew of, when the Chief had remained on duty all night, and all through the next day too, looking his immaculate self late the next evening, in spite of having had no sleep for more than thirty-six hours. What kind of life was it for the other? he wondered. The man who sat at the very centre of the web of secret agents, scattered throughout the world, directing and controlling this empire, giving the necessary orders, having the entire picture filed away in his mind. It was difficult to visualise the kind of outlook, the sort of mind, which the other must have. And the odd thing about it all was that he looked no different from a thousand men one might meet in the streets of London at any hour of the day.

'I suppose that everything will be top priority.'

'I gather that is the case,' nodded the other. 'The Chief, however, does not take me into his full confidence.'

It was a mildly delivered rebuff and Carradine knew better than to keep on plying the other with questions. He would doubtless discover the reasons for his urgent summons in due course.

When they drew up outside the tall building in Regent's Park, the moon was sliding down towards the western horizon, and there was a brightening streak of grey in the other direction, the tops of the building standing out in dark silhouette against the sky.

'I'll take your luggage along to your flat,' said the chauffeur, opening the door for him.

'Thanks.' Carradine got out and stood for a moment on the pavement outside the building, sniffing the air. It was still cold and the smell of the rain was in his nostrils. He thought of the warm, balmy air of the tiny fishing village in Spain, of the great stretch of blue ocean that rolled out to the skyline, of the cloudless skies, and the contrast with what he saw all about him was even more painful.

Inside, he made his way quickly to the room on the fifth floor. From the outside, the room looked no different from all the others in the building which was the Headquarters of the Secret Service; but this was only an external appearance. He knocked loudly on the door, heard the gruff voice bidding him enter, and walked inside, closing the door softly behind him.

'Sit down, Carradine,' said the other, motioning to the chair placed in front of his desk. Like the man who sat behind it, the desk was highly polished, immaculate, and the papers stacked neatly in three piles to the left and one on the right. Even to Carradine's keen gaze, it seemed that they had been meticulously arranged with a millimetric accuracy.

Carradine lowered himself into the chair, crossed his legs and sat back with a faintly audible sigh, forcing himself to relax. He could tell nothing of the nature of the summons from the other's features. The bright, sharp eyes glanced over him,

46

missing nothing. There was a faintly humorous smile on the other's face and Carradine felt an odd tightening of his mind. He could be prepared for anything, he told himself inwardly. Whenever the other's features were creased in that strangely beatific smile, there was something really sickly in store for him. From past experience, he had learned to notice these things.

The Chief cleared his throat, placed the tips of his square-ended fingers together and stared at him over the pyramid they formed. 'You appeared to be having quite a time with yourself at Tamariu. Sorry to have to drag you away from the easy life.'

'That's quite all right, sir. Things change, I suppose.'

'How were things at Tamariu?' The shrewd gaze fixed on Carradine's face.

Damn him, thought the other with a faint sense of irritated surprise, he knows that something happened there, although God alone how.

'A little trouble, sir.'

The Chief's brows went up a little. 'Trouble?'

'There was a girl there at the hotel who — '

'As far as you're concerned, Carradine,' murmured the other softly, 'there usually is. But go on. What proved to be so interesting about her?'

'I'm not sure, sir.' Carradine furrowed his brow a little. This was not going to be an easy thing to put into words. He had the odd feeling that if he went into it in any detail at all, he might find himself sitting behind his desk, spending the next day writing a report on the incident. 'Her name was Francesca Romano. Most of the time she spent at the window of her room watching what was going on along the beach with a pair of high-powered binoculars. She was evidently onto something. Someone tried to kill me with a spear-gun while I was skin-diving and since I thought it possible she might have seen who it was, I asked her about it at dinner. She denied having seen anyone, but I'm sure she was lying.'

'Why would she do that?'

'Again I'm not sure. Unless she didn't want to involve me in what was going on.

I received a clear-cut warning not to probe into things that didn't concern me over the telephone. While I was away, she vanished. I followed her and the last I saw of her, she was being taken out into the bay in a multi-boat. I'd like to have got to the bottom of it, but then your message came and I had to leave.' Carradine grinned wryly. 'If there's one thing I hate, it's leaving something half-done.'

The other's eyes regarded Carradine attentively until he had finished, then he nodded his head sympathetically. 'I understand how you feel. Unfortunately this business has come up and I've had orders from the PM to look into it right away.'

Carradine's nod was taut. It was coming now, he thought to himself.

The Chief was silent for a long moment, watching Carradine speculatively. When he did speak, his question took Carradine by surprise.

'Have you ever wondered what would be one of the most important industrial acquisitions in a time of war, Carradine?'

Carradine shrugged. 'There must be a

49

lot of things, sir,' he said softly. 'Rocket missiles, nuclear fuel.' He searched his mind for others.

The Chief shook his head slowly. 'All of those are important, I'll admit. But the wheels of industry, particularly the specialised industry one must have to fight a modern war, would never turn without diamonds — industrial diamonds. A country needs them by the thousand, possibly by the million. And I think you can realise that a process of manufacturing these diamonds which is both quick and cheap would be of immense value to the country possessing it.'

'But where do we come in, sir?'

'I'll explain that,' the Chief said. 'Throughout the past ten decades or so, several attempts have been made to make artificial diamonds. The five attempts to obtain sufficiently high temperatures and pressures to simulate nature's way of producing diamonds in the Earth's crust ended in disaster, but from one or two of these experiments, rough diamonds were found in the debris. The present process is firmly in the hands of the Oppenheimer Group — at least, they had the secrets of the best, workable method until a little while ago.'

Carradine could feel the tightness coming on again. He had the feeling that the other was getting to the point of his interview. Outside, there was a soft drizzle against the windows and a mist seemed to have developed.

'We stumbled on this quite by accident,' the Chief resumed. 'A member of our scientific delegations to Russia was approached by one of their scientists who wanted to defect to the West. He spoke of the process that he had developed for producing industrial diamonds in large quantities at a cost far less than any process now known. Naturally this report filtered back to us, but we decided to treat it with a great deal of caution. After all, there have been several instances of trouble whenever we sent a delegation to Russia, especially if any member of the delegation speaks the language as fluently as Foster apparently did.'

'Foster?'

'That's right. Foster was the man approached. You see, there was just the chance that someone was hoping to trick him into an indiscreet act. If that happened, there would be the usual arrests, followed by several weeks before our Consul in Moscow could get in touch with him, and then the public trial with a trumped up charge which they would make stick by some means or other. It has happened before and I foresaw that it could well happen again.'

'But you changed your mind, sir.'

'I made more inquiries through one or two of our agents inside Russia about this Professor Ubyenkov. It seems that he has been working on some secret process, but it was impossible to obtain any details about it, other than that it was being financed by the Russian Government. If it does deal with a new and revolutionary method for producing quantities of industrial diamonds, then it is vital that we get this information.'

Carradine nodded his head but said nothing, waiting for the other to go on.

'It has to be done the hard way, I'm afraid.'

'Do we know where Ubyenkov is at the moment?'

'Only vaguely. We know that he isn't in Russia. Three weeks ago, he apparently left the laboratories where he works and managed to give his guards — supervisors, call them what you will — the slip. How he did it we don't know, but you can imagine the unholy flap which followed.'

'I can indeed. A man with that sort of knowledge in his mind would be worth a king's ransom to the West.'

'Exactly. We received this report from one of our men the day before yesterday.' The Chief passed the piece of paper across to Carradine, who read it quickly.

It said: '*Small consignment of gems no longer available. Regret shipped abroad, possibly Black Seven. Will require urgent investigation, other parties interested. Would request contact be re-established as soon as possible.*'

Carradine handed the slip of paper back to the other. The Chief flickered a glance at him, then looked away. 'Black

Seven,' he said softly. 'That's Bulgaria.' He paused for a very long time, then repeated the words softly, expressionlessly, as one would express some strangely powerful occult incantation in the hope that it would ward off something evil and terrifying.

'Bulgaria. That makes things very difficult.'

Carradine sat, saying nothing. This was undoubtedly it, he thought.

'We must get this man out of Bulgaria and back to London,' went on the other quietly. 'I don't care how it's done, but I want him here, you understand.'

'Perfectly, sir. But as you said yourself it isn't going to be easy. Do we have any idea what this man looks like?'

'Nothing much. I've had the man whom he first contacted brought here and he's given something for Jones to come up with using the Identikit. See what you can make of that when you've got a free moment. Unfortunately, Ubyenkov was not one of the men we were interested in until now. We have nothing else on him. About all we do know of him is that his father was killed fighting under General Denikin during the attack on Moscow in October 1919. This, perhaps, would explain why he is willing to come over to the west. It's evident he has no love for the present regime in Russia.'

Carradine gave a quick nod. He cast his mind back to the history of the Russian Revolution and the years immediately following it. His memory was good, but his information of that period sketchy. A little of it came back to him. Stalin had organised the Battle of Orel when the Red Army had halted General Denikin's advance on Moscow and turned the retreat into a counter-offensive. Things had been patched up between the White and Red Armies following the end of the Civil War that had split Russia, but perhaps the old rivalries and enmities still smouldered beneath the surface, the old wounds not fully healed.

'Do we have anyone in Bulgaria I could contact?'

The chief nodded. 'Man called Volescu. He's a good man. You can trust him completely. He's been working for us since before the war. The Reds were somewhat suspicious of him when they marched into Bulgaria, but since then he's managed to keep them off his trail.'

'But it's unlikely that he knows where Ubyenkov may be hiding out?'

'Afraid so. Wherever he is, you can be sure he is well hidden, and there must be someone helping him stay out of sight. From what we know of conditions inside Bulgaria, their big Red cousins have only to put on the squeeze, diplomatic or otherwise, and they go out of their way to find men like Ubyenkov and hand him back. The flap over the U2 incident was one thing, and the corresponding flap over this will be of a similar sort of magnitude. They simply can't afford to let him slip through their fingers and reach the West with everything he knows of this process.' The chief pointed a finger at the message on the desk. 'You can see from that, that they have already put the machinery into motion. They will have several of their best men on the look-out for him, tracking down every clue. I'm afraid I'm really throwing you in at the deep end this time, but perhaps you can see how vital it is that you get out there as soon as possible, even though it did mean breaking up your holiday.'

The smile on the other's face did not touch his eyes. Sitting back, he linked his fingers together, then pushed the button on his desk. In answer to the faint look of inquiry on Carradine's face, he said: 'You may have heard from Wilson that I've been up all night, working on the reports which have been coming through in a constant stream. I'm going to have a coffee now. Would you like some, or is it whisky for you?'

'Bourbon — straight, sir,' said Carradine.

'So be it,' nodded the other. When the drinks came, he settled himself back in his seat and stared moodily at the cup of coffee. At length, he said: 'This isn't going to be an easy business. Still you know that already, I suppose. Any ideas yet how you're going to go about it?'

'Nothing definite as yet, sir. I'd like a little time in which to think this thing out. At the moment, I'm afraid I can't see much beyond getting in touch with this man Volescu. A lot is going to depend on what he can tell me — if anything. It's obvious that Ubyenkov has slipped across the frontier somewhere and I guess that a man in his position, secluded in some laboratory for most of his life, just isn't the sort of man who would know what to do when it comes to getting past frontier guards. He has evidently had help of some kind and it's just possible that Volescu has contacts who may be able to discover something about this.'

'It's possible,' nodded the other. 'But equally so, if he has, then so have the Red agents and they're a little closer to things in Bulgaria than we are. They have the edge on us this time I'm afraid and if I'm quite honest with you, I can't see Ubyenkov staying free for very long unless we get to him in time. Even then, you have to convince anyone close to him that you're not a Russian agent playing a double game.'

'You make it all sound so very straightforward, sir,' said Carradine dryly. He finished the whisky and set his glass down. 'When do you want me to leave?'

The Chief lifted his head and laid a stern glance on Carradine. 'It will have to be soon, I'm afraid. Shall we say the day after tomorrow? Give you a few hours in London. Then it's the flight to Sofia for you.'

Carradine nodded, then knit his brow in sudden thought.

The Chief noticed the look at once, said: 'Something on your mind?'

'I'm wondering why he made for Bulgaria. Surely it would have been easier for him to have slipped across into Romania. He must have crossed the frontier around Izmail or Reni, then move through Dobrogea and into Bulgaria around Silistra. Seems to me to be a dangerous and roundabout route to take when he could have gone directly into Romania.'

The other's eyes had suddenly turned speculative. 'I suppose he had a reason for doing things that way. Probably he had friends in Bulgaria whereas there was no one he could trust in Romania. Whatever the answer, you have all the information available to me. If I learn anything further within the next thirty-six hours I'll see to it that you get it. In the meantime, if I were you, I'd check up on everything there is to know about that part of the world. Also, look in on Jones and see what the Identikit shows. You might also want to have a word with Forbes.' The Chief's face looked grim. 'He has one or two ideas he wants to put into practice and I'd say you're just the usual suspect he's looking for.'

Carradine rose lithely to his feet. The interview was obviously over. He knew it was possible he would not see the other again before leaving for Sofia. He had been given his instructions and now it was up to him to carry them out to the best of his ability.

* * *

After leaving the office, he made his way first to the room on the second floor, knocked, pushed open the door and went inside. There was a man seated behind the low desk in one corner of the room and his face broke into a smile as he said: 'Thought you'd be along as soon as you'd had a talk with the Old Man. I suppose you want to take a look at Professor Ubyenkov as we see him.'

'That's why I'm here,' Carradine said. He had always had, at the back of his mind, a vague distrust of the Identikit. It seemed all too pat to be really true. This building up of a picture from scattered pieces of information. How close it really came to a person's true identity, he wasn't sure about. But at the moment it was all they had to go on and anything was better than nothing at all. The picture that they built up for him might possibly eliminate half of the population of Bulgaria.

'All right, let's take a look at my pigeon.' He seated himself in the chair near the desk as the other swivelled in his seat, snapped on a switch and gave a nod towards the face that flicked on the apparatus. Carradine eyed it closely. Reasonably ordinary, damnit, he thought inwardly. Nothing outwardly to go on, which might make this man stand out in a crowd — and there was, of course, always a possibility that he was sufficiently frightened to have tried to alter his appearance, knowing that there would be Red agents hot on his trail at any moment.

'Not too much to go on, I'm afraid,' murmured Jones apologetically. 'This is about as close as we can get with this machine.'

'And how much faith do you put in it?'

The other shrugged, then forced a quick smile. He said cheerfully: 'I can see from your expression that you're not too taken with it.'

'Not really. Only had to use it once. Gave me a completely wrong picture of my man. If I'd taken it as gospel, I'd have been arrested for going after the head of one of our biggest banking concerns. But I suppose it's better than nothing. This is put together from what that science delegate brought back?'

'That's right,' agreed Jones. 'Naturally, I'd have preferred to have had some corroboration from other witnesses, but it seems that the professor did not want to trust too many people. Seems that Foster was the only man he approached, the only one who saw him.'

'Then this will have to do.' Carradine glanced again at the picture on the Identikit, impressing it on his mind. The balding head with the wide, square features so characteristically Russian, but with the faint look of a dreamer about it too. He could visualise this man working in a laboratory, smouldering inwardly against the badgering of a bureaucratic government, poking its nose into everything that went on, directing and ordering, making it virtually impossible for a research scientist to get on with his job. Such a man could not be rushed, could not be ordered about, if he was to give his best. Sometimes Carradine wondered how the Russians ever got any original research work done at all. Certainly, they were good copyists, and they had had the benefit of the German and Czech scientists whom they had taken back with them during the first few weeks following the end of the war when a great many of the top European men had vanished without trace, only to turn up later in Russia. Gradually, it was true, they were now beginning to realise that they were behind the rest of the world in original research and were doing their best to catch up.

He felt a little sense of grim amusement. The Russian scientists had one big incentive to work, which the Western men did not have: the threat of extinction if they failed in their task.

'Well now, have you got everything you want from me?' Jones asked as Carradine got up from his chair.

'I think so. If anything else comes to me in the next day or so, I'll drop in and have another talk.'

'Certainly, any time,' nodded the other. He flicked off the switch.

Leaving Jones, Carradine debated whether to return to his flat and get something to eat, or whether to pay a call on Forbes. In the end, he decided to get something to eat first, have a bath and then come back. After all, his watch said that it was still before nine o'clock. He had plenty of time in which to make his preparations and he did not think very well on an empty stomach.

He returned to Headquarters shortly after eleven o'clock. The drizzle had given way to a broken-cloud sky, with occasional brief rays of sunlight streaking the pavements and buildings. Determined to keep in condition, he had walked it back from his flat, a matter of a mile and a half through crowded London streets.

Forbes was a small, meek-looking man, with a pair of rimless glasses perched precariously on the edge of his nose. He had a habit of continually peering over them, as though they were for the benefit of his nose and not his eyes. It seemed incredible, looking at him, that he was in charge of one of the most up-to-date and varied arsenals in the whole country. It was doubtful, Carradine reflected, as he let himself into the room, whether any collection such as this existed anywhere else in the world, although he had not seen the Russian counterpart which, rumour had it, existed within a stone's throw of the Kremlin in Moscow.

Forbes glanced up at Carradine with a hint of conspiracy in his smile.

'Heard you might be giving me a visit,' he said genially, nodding towards a chair. 'I gather you will be out of the country for a little time.'

'That's right.' Carradine nodded. 'The Chief thinks you may have something of interest for me.' He doubted if the other knew his destination. That was probably something known only to the Chief and perhaps PM.

'Cigarette?' The other fished in his pocket, withdrew the slender gold case, offered a cigarette to the other, then snapped the case shut again.

'Thanks.' Carradine lit the other's cigarette and then his own.

Forbes still held the case in his right hand. He said softly: 'Quite an interesting thing, this.' He held it out. 'You'll notice the monogram.'

Carradine leaned forward and took the cigarette case. On the front, worked into the metal, was a crest and the initials S. C. underneath. 'Why does it have my initials on it?' he asked curiously.

Forbes took it back without answering, then placed his forefinger over the raised initials and twisted it sharply to the left. There was a faint, almost inaudible click and a six-inch blade of a knife slid from the top of the case, the metal gleaming in the light.

'One of our weapons.' Forbe's voice had taken on a fresh briskness. 'The knife blade is based on a telescopic principle but it's quite deadly all the same. Better handle it carefully until you get used to it. I wouldn't want you to injure yourself.' His smile widened. 'Here's something else to go with it.'

The lighter looked quite ordinary. With a feeling of trepidation, Carradine flicked it down. For a moment, he looked surprised as the wheel merely rasped on the flint and it lit first time. Brows raised, he glanced up.

Forbes took it from him. 'If you press the other lever,' he explained, 'this is what happens.' Holding it a little distance from him, he pressed down on the other side of the level mechanism. There was no sound at all as it depressed under his thumb, but a thin jet of liquid shot into the air. There was no smell but almost at once, Carradine felt his eyes begin to water and the sharp stinging sensation almost blinded him. He took an involuntary step backward.

'If that jet had hit your eyes it would have temporarily blinded you and also put you completely out of action for an hour or so. It's a mixture of one of the latest tear gases and a nerve gas which our men have recently developed. Quite harmless in the long run, but extremely efficient.'

Gingerly, Carradine took the lighter and slipped it into his pocket. 'Do you have any more delightful playthings?' he asked.

Forbes nodded briefly. For a moment, the meek look vanished and there was a hard, cunning expression in his eyes. 'I think we can pride ourselves on keeping just one jump ahead of the Reds when it comes to designing and producing weapons of protection and destruction. Let me show you the latest range we have. If there's anything that takes your fancy, I'm

sure we can let you have it — and
quickly.'

A little over an hour later, Carradine
left the tiny room at the rear of the
building. He had the odd feeling that
maybe a man like Forbes, so utterly out
of character according to his external
appearance, might manage things better
than he would. Who would have thought
that a man like Forbes worked with these
deadly pieces of machinery, these
delicately-figured mechanisms that could
destroy a man within seconds, or put
him out of action without him ever
knowing that he was in deadly danger.

He took the lift to his office on the
sixth floor, spent the rest of the afternoon
behind his desk, working on the reports
that were furnished for him, learning by
heart all the details of this case. By the
time it was night, he had most of it in his
head and knew what he was up against.
As he walked through the darkening
streets to his flat, he was already turning
over ideas in his mind.

3

DARKNESS IN THE CITY

The clamour of the aircraft's engines was still echoing in Carradine's ears as he made his way across to the customs bay at the airport. He had seen the lights of Sofia down below him as they had circled the city before coming in to land and a faint sense of nostalgia went through him. It was now several years since he had last been in the city. Doubtless many things would have changed since those days.

Everything he carried on him was examined by the customs official. He felt a sense of grim amusement as they went through his luggage. It was an acid test for the weapons that Forbes had given him before he left England that none of them was suspected. There were the two bottles of whisky, placed carefully, but not too carefully, at the bottom of this case. The man took them out, turned one over in his hands for a long moment and sniffed it appreciatively, cocked an eye in Carradine's direction and said something rapidly in Bulgarian before putting it back and snapping down the middle of the case, scrolling some squiggle in chalk on top of it and sliding it towards him over the counter.

Passing through into the lounge, he looked about him. He had not liked the look of the customs official back there. A suspicious man. His eyes and face gave him away. Someone who distrusted everything Western, and yet he had the feeling that if he could have got him alone, away from any chance of hidden microphones and the like, the other would have plied him with questions about England and western Europe. It had been the same whenever he had been in Russia, he recalled; everyone wanted to know of England but talked little of their own country. In Russia, he remembered, every block, every building, had its own watchdog, who reported on everything that happened, who watched any foreigners who might go into a private flat.

Almost certainly, it was the same here.

The man who stood leaning against the wall ten yards from the entrance to the airport was short and dark, with a thin, ferret-shaped face. He gave Carradine a quick glance, then sidled forward silently and pointed to the car which stood at the kerb a short distance away.

'I was told to meet you here,' he said in halting English. 'I'll take your case.'

Without bothering to ask Carradine his name, the other took the case from him, marched in front of him along the street, let the case drop into the back of the battered old car, then opened the door and motioned Carradine inside. Shrugging, the other lowered his head and seated himself. The springs creaked ominously under his weight and repeated their performance as the driver got in and started up the engine with a quick jab of his forefinger at the start button. The engine coughed, spluttered, then started up, the ancient car vibrating in every bolt and seam, shaking like a man with the ague.

They moved away from the pavement,

out into the desultory stream of traffic, all of which seemed to be moving in one direction. Very soon, they moved down a modern street, wider than Carradine remembered from his previous visit.

'Are we going straight to Volescu?' Carradine asked as the silence grew long.

The driver shook his head. 'Volescu thought that you would need some rest after your flight here. I'm to take you to one of the hotels and then pick you up in the morning. Ten o'clock exactly. Please remember. It is important that we leave Sofia. We have a long distance to travel and although everything is peaceful and quiet at the moment, we don't want anyone sniffing around and following us.'

'Then Volescu doesn't live in Sofia?'

'No, we must go to Kazanluk. That is about a hundred and seventy kilometres east of here. Sometimes there are roadblocks set up and for the past two weeks, maybe a little longer, there has been a tightening of controls in eastern Bulgaria.' He shot Carradine a sudden, quizzical glance. 'Perhaps that is why you are here, eh?'

'Perhaps.' Carradine nodded. Inwardly, he was turning this fresh piece of information over in his mind. Road blocks and a tightening up of the checks made on traffic moving around eastern Bulgaria pointed to the Reds knowing that Professor Ubyenkov was in that area. No doubt the Soviet agents were moving in quickly, trying to find him before he could slip through the Iron Curtain to the West.

He was booked in at a hotel in one of the narrow streets, set some distance from the main residential area of the city. Whether it had been chosen deliberately so that he might remain unobtrusively out of sight, he could not tell. Very likely this had been done on the orders of Anton Volescu. But the hotel was certainly not one of the most comfortable he had known.

Early the next morning, he was awake, staring about the dingy room into which he had been shown the previous evening. It had been late when they had arrived there, but nevertheless he felt oddly refreshed after his six-hour sleep. Pulling aside the heavy curtains that successfully blotted out every trace of daylight, he stared down into the narrow cobbled street outside. At first, it appeared to be deserted in the grey light. Then his keen-eyed gaze fastened on the dark shadow which lay between two of the buildings on the other side of the street. Had it been his imagination, or had that really been a slight movement there, back in the shadow — the sort of movement a man might make easing a cramped leg after standing for some time watching the windows of the hotel? He edged back a little, keeping the curtains parted. He felt sweat on his forehead and resisted the urge to wipe it away with the back of his hand.

Nothing for several moments, then he caught the brief yellow-orange flare of a match being struck on the wall, and the red glow of a cigarette tip as the silent watcher dragged the smoke down into his lungs. He was being watched, Carradine thought grimly. But by whom? Who else but Volescu and his men knew of his presence in Sofia? Possibly it was one of

Volescu's men, making sure he was not disturbed; all laid on courtesy of the Bulgarian section of the Secret Service. But a little voice at the back of his mind warned him that this was unlikely to be the case. The chauffeur had said he would be there at precisely ten o'clock. It was unlikely he would come before then.

He waited for ten minutes while the man standing in the shadows smoked his cigarette. Then the other stepped out into the open and gave the front of the hotel a quick look that missed nothing. For several seconds his gaze seemed to dwell on Carradine's window and he had the strange feeling that the other had X-ray eyes which could probe right through the thick curtains in front of him, could see him standing there looking down. Then, turning his gaze away, the man walked off along the narrow street, feet making no sound on the cobbles, his shoulders hunched forward a little, his soft hat pulled well down over his face, hiding his features completely.

Carradine dawdled in his room for over an hour. Then he took out the Luger from its small case and slid the firing mechanism back and forth experimentally for a time, admiring the battered smoothness with which it worked before clicking the magazine into place beside the butt. Going downstairs, he went into the small dining room, picked himself a table against the wall where he could watch the door, and smoked a cigarette while waiting for the waiter to put in an appearance. If he knew anything about these small Balkan hotels, the service was extremely bad and slow.

He had been there for four minutes, with the cigarette smoked down almost to the end, when one of the doors inside the room opened and a waiter stepped through. He gave the tables a perfunctory glance, noticed Carradine sitting there and came forward, a faint look of surprise on his face.

'I'm sorry, sir,' he said in full English, evidently recognising Carradine from the previous night. 'I did not know that anyone would be down solely for breakfast.' His tone implied that only Englishmen were sufficiently mad to want anything to eat at this unearthly hour of the morning.

Carradine gave him a tight-lipped smile. 'Am I too early? I thought that — '

'Oh, not at all, sir.' The other dragged out his syllables with a faint leer that made Carradine feel nauseous. 'I'll get you something right away.'

Carradine had time in which to wonder what sort of something he would get before the other returned, but when the meal was spread out before him, he was pleasantly surprised. It was then that he realised that the continental European had justice on his side when he claimed that British food was not worth the effort of eating. The cheese was firm yet had a buttery consistency, and tasted delicious; the bowl of mixed figs and dates held just the right tang to set the muscles at the side of his jaw stinging. He finished with a freshly roasted coffee, then sat back and enjoyed a second cigarette. Carradine had been glad to find that the coffee was black and strong. A quick glance at his watch told him it was almost eight o'clock. The sun had risen but was still hidden behind a bank of hazy cloud low in the east, and the light over the city was still grey.

Going back to his room, he checked through everything that Forbes had pressed on him before he had left. How many of these fiendish devices would he have to use before this mission was over? he wondered tensely. Whatever happened, it was essential that he continued to think ahead, to trust no one. This man Anton Volescu. What did he know about him? Virtually nothing but what the Chief had told him. Perhaps, of all the men he would meet here, he was the only one he could really trust.

He sat down on the edge of the bed, where he could just look down onto the street whenever he straightened himself up and lifted his head. Now there was nothing for him to do but sit and wait until ten o'clock. Then there would be the long drive east to Kazanluk. He tried to recall his geography of this region. If his memory did not fail him, Kazanluk lay just south of the Balkan Mountains. The towns en route would be Novoselci,

Zlatica, Karlovo, Shipka and then Kazan-luk.

Punctually at ten o'clock, he was waiting just inside the small foyer of the hotel. The street was empty with no sound of the car. Glancing down at his wristwatch, he eyed the red second sweep hand. Two minutes past ten. Something was wrong. He knew enough of these men to realise that in their business, minutes were of vital importance. He placed his right hand in his pocket and fingered the butt of the Luger. It felt cold and reassuring.

Five past ten. He dropped the butt of his cigarette onto the ground and glanced up at the sound of a car entering the street. Five seconds later, the car turned the corner and came to a stop directly opposite him. The thin-faced chauffeur opened the door from the inside, took his case and dropped it into the back seat, waited until he was seated beside him, then let in the clutch and drove quickly along the street, around the corner and into the main thoroughfare. They swung around a sharp S-bend, heading towards the eastern outskirts of Sofia.

Minutes later they were out of most of the traffic, and ten seconds after cutting over a low bridge they swung out of the city, the driver putting his foot down on the accelerator. The car creaked and groaned, but on the dashboard the needle of the speedometer rose slowly until it touched the ninety mark. His forehead furrowed in thought, Carradine glanced out of the corner of his eye at the man seated beside him. The other seemed relaxed, hands gripping the steering wheel, but there was a tightness about the corners of his mouth, about the set of the jaw and the narrowed eyes.

Was the other stepping on the accelerator to make up for those few lost minutes, determined to be on time at the other end of the journey if not at the beginning? Or had there been trouble back there? Turning his head, he looked behind him through the rear window. Nothing following them. The road behind them was clear for two miles in the bright sunlight that now flooded over the countryside.

He shrugged, turned back, and settled

himself deeper into his seat. The back of the seat was hard and uncomfortable against his shoulder blades and it occurred to him that he would have a sore posterior before the time they reached their destination. As for the car itself, it had turned out to be something of a surprise to him. Outwardly, it looked like a pre-war model, possibly capable of a good turn of speed in its prime, but now long past that. Only the smooth purring of the engine gave the lie to that; the red needle of the speedometer was now hovering close to the hundred mark. There was probably a very special kind of engine tucked away under the bonnet, he mused, and that red switch on the edge of the dashboard was, in all probability, a supercharger. Trust a man like Volescu to have a car like this.

They had driven for perhaps five kilometres before the driver eased his foot from the accelerator pedal, letting the engine idle, the speedometer needle dropping back to seventy. The car had excellent road-handling properties, in spite of the uneven nature of the road in places, especially on the bends.

'How long before we reach Kazanluk?' Carradine asked without turning his head.

The driver pursed his lips. 'Another two hours. The road becomes dangerous a little further east and there are places when we skirt the mountains where we must be careful of landslides.'

'I see.' The other's tone had been such as not to invite any further questions, but Carradine persisted. 'And back there in Sofia. What happened to make you late? I understood that Volescu always believed in absolute punctuality.'

'There was a little difficulty,' said the other harshly. 'It was nothing for you to worry about, something readily taken care of. We are used to handling this sort of thing.'

'Trouble?' asked Carradine brutally. He could see by the look on the other's face that he did not want to talk about it, that he considered it to be none of Carradine's business. But damnit all, it *was* his business, he told himself fiercely. After all, it was his life these men were playing with, as well as their own.

'A little,' admitted the chauffeur finally. He bit the words out in sharp, staccato syllables.

'The Reds?'

'Perhaps. It is difficult to be sure. There are many different factions inside Bulgaria. Some are in this business only for the money, others do not care whether or not they are paid for what they do. These are the dangerous ones who kill for the sheer sadistic joy of it. I kill too, but only because I believe that the cause for which I am fighting is the right one.'

Carradine nodded, deciding that the man was what was known as a patriot. He felt a tight sense of a grim amusement. He had heard all this before, not once but many times. It was the usual call that went out whenever any country wanted war. Hitler had used it, and Mussolini, and if one were really honest about this, so had Churchill and Roosevelt. The rallying call. Our cause is just. God is with us. It made one a little sick after a while.

There were several moments of silence.

The other eased forward gently on the accelerator. The car moved forward, eating up the kilometres. For most of the way the road was deserted. Somehow, Carradine had expected more traffic on it. After all, it was one of the main roads east from the capital. Perhaps there was very little petrol to be had for private motoring.

He looked at his watch. A little after ten-thirty. They topped a low rise, then drove down into Novoselci, passed through it and increased the speed once more. The forests closed in on them now, stretching down onto both sides of the road. In places, the trees joined overhead, their branches forming in effect an impenetrable carpet of leaves that shut out the sunlight, but kept in the heat.

The driver touched a switch, there was a faint grating sound above Carradine's head, and part of the car roof slid back, bringing a welcome touch of cooler air. He drew it down deeply into his lungs, nodding obliquely at the other. The driver kept the car at about seventy, and now that the roof was open there was a wind roar that made talking difficult, if not impossible.

They came out of the shade of the forest into more open country with the tall mountains, snow-covered on their crests, crowding down on them. This was the real Bulgaria. Sofia was all right, but he much preferred to be out here. There were new chalets high on these mountains where one could ski and get away from everything.

Turning his head, he glanced back through the rear window, back to where the first Teutonic forest was receding into the distance. The road that wound away back there was still deserted — no, there was one car on it, far back in the distance, but coming up fast. A red car, he noticed — a bright, garish spot of colour against the otherwise green and sombre background.

'It looks as though you're about to be challenged,' he remarked to the other.

The driver slid his gaze towards the mirror for an instant. The expression on his face did not seem to change, yet there was a change, something subtle that

Carradine noticed. Fear, or apprehension? It could have been either. Carradine was not sure.

Reaching forward, the driver flicked up the switch that Carradine has spotted a little earlier. The shrill, shrieking whine of the blowers from the supercharger screeched in his ears. The car leapt forward, shuddering a little. The ground on either side of the road lost its detail and dissolved into a blur of green and brown anonymity. The red needle climbed swiftly. Ninety-five, a hundred, a hundred and ten. It was still climbing, but glancing behind him, Carradine saw that the red car was still gaining on them, slowly but quite perceptibly.

'You think it may be trouble?' he asked quietly.

'It's possible. No one in their right mind would drive a car like that along this road unless they had a very good reason for it, or they were not caring whether they lived or died.'

Switching his gaze to the road ahead of them, Carradine saw the reason for the other's remark. They were almost at the end of a long, ten-kilometre stretch of straight road. Now they were entering a system of sharply-angled bends and switch back curves where they would be forced to slow down or run the very grave risk of going over the edge. In places, there was a sheer drop of almost two hundred metres on the left-hand side of the road; and at the speed they were going it needed only a slight mistake on the part of the driver, a swerve which could not be instantly controlled, and they would plunge, cartwheeling, down the sheer slope and finish up in a mass of tangled, twisted metal at the bottom. He did not relish their chances of survival if that happened.

The driver touched the brakes, lightly at first, then with more pressure. The car slowed. He snapped off the supercharger switch and the howl of the blowers died at once, leaving only the wind blast in their ears.

A quick glance over his shoulder showed Carradine that the red car had almost caught up with them. Its speed must have been quite fantastic to have covered so much ground in so short a time. He tried to make out the shapes of the men inside but the sunlight was glinting fiercely on the curved windscreen and in the glare of eye-searing brilliance, he could make out nothing. The car was about three hundred metres behind them, closing only slowly now.

Narrowing his eyes, Carradine tried to make out the features of the two men seated in the other car. There was that tight, tensed-up feeling back in the pit of his stomach and acting on impulse, he drew the Luger from his pocket and thumbed off the safety catch.

'Just in case they do mean trouble,' he said quietly, throwing a quick, sideways glance at the other.

He saw the man give a brief nod, saw the tightening of his lips. 'They probably know the road as well as I do,' he grunted. 'But we may be able to shake them off three kilometres further on. There is a tunnel there and they will not be able to speed through it for fear of running into the back of us.'

Unless they decided to make their play

before then, Carradine reflected. But no, there was no sign the car was closing up. They were maintaining their distance. Perhaps he was doing them an injustice. Maybe they were just a couple of men out for a quiet drive through this beautiful countryside, with no thought of violence in their heads. Maybe!

The Bulgarian threw the heavy car around the corners, keeping his foot resting lightly on the accelerator, ready to thrust down on it hard when they reached the mouth of the tunnel. Inwardly, Carradine hoped that the other knew what he was doing. If those two men in the car were Red agents, they would not be biding their time without a reason. They would know the tunnel lay directly ahead, and they were prepared for anything the driver might do. The one thing that they might not be prepared for was the gun in Carradine's right fist, his finger tight on the trigger.

'There we are,' said the driver softly. He nodded his head towards the windscreen. Carradine shifted his glance away from the car behind them for a second.

The steep slope of the mountains crowded down on to the road directly in front of them and less than half a kilometre away he saw the gaping black mouth of the tunnel, looming up on them in the bright, glaring sunlight. There was a shallow S-bend in the road and they were on the straight. The second he came out of the bend, the driver thrust down on the accelerator. The car lurched forward as though propelled from a gun. Ten seconds and the sunlight was gone, blotted out by the tunnel walls.

Far-off in the distance, it was just possible to see the round circle of daylight that marked the other end of the tunnel. For the men following behind, there would be only blackness, that tiny circle of light blotted out by the massive bulk of their own car. But the driver simply pointed the bonnet of the car directly at it, and gave it all it had.

The beating roar of the powerful engine was flung at them from the curved tunnel walls, magnified a hundred times, howling in their ears. Then, as the end of the tunnel rushed up on them, the whine turned into an ear-shattering roar that lasted for the barest fraction of a second. Bright sunlight struck them forcibly. Carradine blinked his eyes several times to adjust them to the glare. For a few seconds, there was a red haze dancing in front of his vision. Then he was able to see properly. The round disc of the sun was in front of them now, in the cloudless blue-white of the heavens. How the driver managed to make out details of the road ahead of him was nothing short of a miracle. Yet their car kept to the road, hugging the smooth surface as it plunged down the winding mountain road, which twisted down from the tunnel towards the valley between the shoulders of the tall ridges. Through the haze, there was also the added glare of sunlight reflected from the sparkling white collars of snow that covered the upper peaks. Down below them, perhaps three hundred metres away, the road rapidly gave up. There was a sign by the side of the road, but they had come upon then flashed by it so quickly that he did not have the time to see what it was meant to indicate. A quick spin of the wheel and they made a corner on two wheels, cut along a straight stretch like a bat out of hell, then were forced to slow as they drove through the cobbled streets of a small village which suddenly materialised out of nowhere at the bottom of the slope. Carradine had a quick, vague impression of a tall-spired church, several houses with steep-sloping roofs clustered around, and then they were out, the driver swiftly changing gears as they laboured up a steep slope.

Behind them, there was no sign of the red car. Had they lost it somewhere along that twisting road? Had there been no connection between it and themselves? Had it simply turned off along one of the few side roads, which branched away into the mountains on either side?

He leaned forward and lit a cigarette. Despite the open roof, the atmosphere in the car was hot and oppressive. Did it always get as hot as this in this area at this time of the year? He thrust the thought away as a roar intruded on his senses from behind. The red car was there, almost on their tail!

The driver gave a sudden warning shout as he glanced into the mirror. He tried to kick a further ounce of speed from the car. But whatever it was that the other car had, it was too much for them. It swerved out to the other side of the road, drew level with them, and then moved on past. Out of the corner of his eye, Carradine saw the tight face, goggles pulled down over the eyes to shield them from the wind stream. The gun cradled in the man's hands was lining up on them as Carradine lifted the Luger. The danger of their position emptied his mind of all other thought. Swiftly, he squeezed the trigger, feeling the heavy gun kick at his wrists. The windscreen shattered as two slugs passed through it. He saw the gunmen flinch as one of the slugs tore into his shoulder. Then the automatic weapon opened fire on them. The brief flare of the muzzle-fire, even in the bright sunlight. The rest of the windscreen vanished as bullets ploughed into the toughened glass. Instinctively, Carradine ducked to one side. The car lurched and dimly, he was aware of his companion slumping forward over the steering column, the dark crimson stain showing through on the brown shirt.

The red car was streaking away along the sunlit road. A bend showed ahead and even as he dropped the Luger on to the floor of the car and reached sideways to grab at the wheel, thrusting the other's body to one side, he knew he was going to be too late, that there was nothing he could do to prevent them from going over.

Desperately, exerting all of his strength in one last, muscle-cracking heave, he sought to keep the car on the road, to thrust his leg forward under the other's body for the brake. The edge of the road came up, spun beneath the churning wheels of the car, and then they were over the side, sliding down the slope, powdery soil flying in a grey-brown cloud all about the car, obscuring details almost completely.

Two short, slender-trunked saplings that barred the way were instantly brushed aside as the bonnet ploughed into them, snapping them off at their bases. There was the first appalling crash as the car struck an upthrusting rock, then bounced for several yards before hammering down on its iron belly in a stretch of soft earth that succeeded in breaking it before it had a chance to turn over. Then, just when it seemed to him that he was going to be all right, the outside wheel hit a sharp rock. There was a loud explosion of a bursting tyre and the car slewed round sharply, tilted onto its side and slid the remaining twenty metres with an ear-splitting screech of tortured metal being abraded by sand and rock. It came to rest abruptly as it hit a mass of rock and dirt. Unable to stop himself, Carradine went forward. His head hit the edge of the dashboard and he went out.

When he came to, the sunlight was glaring blindingly into his eyes. With a tremendous effort, he struggled up from the depths of a black, trance-like unconsciousness that tried to retain its grip on him in spite of everything he could do to snap out of it. Momentarily, he would drag himself up above the surface of consciousness, only to slide back into the deep, terrible darkness again. But gradually, these fleeting moments of awareness were lengthening. Although his mind tried to slip back just when he thought he had it, there was a feeling of something at the back of his mind which grew perceptibly stronger; something to hang on to while he strove to orientate himself.

At last he forced his eyes open again, made himself keep them open, then heaved himself up into a sitting position. There was redness in front of his eyes and several seconds elapsed before he realised that it was his own blood flowing from a gash across his forehead. He put his hand up to it and winced involuntarily as a stab of pain glanced through his skull from front to back.

There was a long moment's silence, a moment in which Carradine was increasingly aware of a sharp-smelling acrid smoke that stung his nostrils and made his eyes run, blurring his vision still further. Turning his head, he stared down into the wide-eyed face, lips bloodless, stretched back over his teeth. The man

had died hard, but almost instanta-
neously. There were at least six bullet
holes in his chest and the steering wheel
had not improved matters either.

He twisted around again, tried to see
where the smoke was coming from. The
metal of the car was blisteringly hot to the
touch and the door next to him had been
buckled out of shape by the force of the
crash. For fifteen seconds, he struggled
with it, and then gave it up. Nothing short
of a crowbar and plenty of leverage would
open that, he decided.

How long had he been out? He glanced
at his watch. The glass was smashed and
both hands had been snapped. He could
have been unconscious for minutes or
hours, there was no way of telling. Was
there any way of getting himself out of
this wreck? And even if he did, where
could he make for? Follow the road and
hope he could reach some small village
where he might be able to get help, get his
injuries tended to? Leaning to one side,
bending over the body of the man
sprawled behind the shattered ruins of the
steering wheel, he twisted his head back

with a powerful wrench of neck muscles and glanced up in the direction of the road. For a moment, he could make out nothing in the all-pervading glare. Then he sucked in a sharp breath and let it go in a slow whistle. There was a car up there, parked on the very edge of the road, and someone was getting out of it, pointing down at him. For a second he had the impression that it was the red car that had come back, its occupants determined to finish the job, to make sure he was dead.

But no, this was a blue car, sleek and shiny, and the figure that had stepped to the edge of the chasm and pointed was a girl. He could just make out the handkerchief she had tied over her hair, fluttering a little behind her in the wind. Then someone else moved to join her, tall, square-shouldered. The man began to clamber carefully down the rocky slope, finding footholds and handholds where none seemed to exist. In places, it seemed impossible that a fly could have come down that slope, yet he seemed to be finding it without difficulty.

The man reached the car, peered in through the shattered windscreen, gave the driver a cursory glance, muttered something in Bulgarian which Carradine did not understand, then caught hold of the top of the door with both of his hands. Leaning back, he wrenched at the tough metal. For a long moment, nothing happened. There was a faint sheen of sweat on the giant's forehead now. His lips were pressed tightly over his clenched teeth and his eyes were mere slits as he exerted all of his strength. Slowly, the metal gave. There was a sudden savage screech as the hinges gave, then the door was pulled back and the man stood looking down at him. Gingerly, Carradine tried to move his legs, and found to his surprise that although there was a stabbing pain of cramp in the muscles of the back of his thighs, he had no broken bones.

Reaching in, the man caught him by the arm, helped him out, and aided him to stand. The full heat of the sun struck him forcibly. A lunging automaton, he somehow managed to stay upright as the other forced him to move away from the car. The smell of smoke was still clinging to the dusty air, still stung his nostrils and the back of his throat. Coughing, the throbbing ache hammering away like a series of tiny trip-hammers behind his skull, he dug in his heels and moved up the slope. There was a sudden feeling behind him, something that he could not identify but would seem to have some important bearing on what was happening. The next second, he went over sideways. He did not fall, but was thrust into the hot dirt by the tremendous weight of the man beside him, held there as that wreck, less than twenty metres away, suddenly retched smoke and erupted in a gush of petrol-driven flame that engulfed it completely. The blast of hot air struck his scalp and he felt the wave of heat push at his body as he lay there with all the wind knocked out of his lungs. Seconds after the ferocious blast, the man on top of him eased his way to one side and got heavily to his feet.

Sobbing breath down into his aching

lungs, Carradine lay with his face pressed into the ground. If only the other would leave him alone, let him live there until some of the life and feeling came back into his battered body. He felt as if he could close his eyes and drift off into sleep — or would it be unconsciousness — again. A hand gripped his arm and tightened, the fingers biting into the flesh with a steel-like strength. Cursing feebly, he got to his feet, swayed, and would have fallen had it not been for the man thrusting him up the slope and propelling him with an urgency that brooked no denial. Carradine ran his fingers through sweat-matted hair, felt the spot where blood has encrusted itself on his lacerated flesh, and sucked in a sharp breath as the pain went through him again. He was in pretty bad shape. Somehow he remained upright, clambering over the razor-edged rocks, moving as nearly as possible along a stretch of earth where the car, when it had plunged down the side of the road, had gouged out a smooth rut in the ground.

Lurching drunkenly, the man beside

him still retaining his grip on his arm, they somehow struggled to the top. Carradine felt himself being thrust over the lip of the road and was dimly aware of the woman moving towards him, reaching down to help him.

Carradine felt the sharp-edged rocks tear into his knee as he was hauled forward. He looked up. The face bending over him was one he recognised. The pale hair rippled over her shoulders, blown a little in the wind, and a stray wisp had fallen over the deep violet eyes that looked down at him with an expression of concern in them. How in hell had she got here?

'Francesca!' He managed to get her name out. 'How in God's name did you come to be here?'

'There's no time for talk now, Steve,' she said urgently. 'Can you walk to the car, or will Carl carry you?'

'Like hell he will,' protested Carradine feebly. Somehow, he made a faint grin. 'I can make it on my own two feet.' He moved towards the car, the big man moving ponderously beside him, opening the door for him. Then he was sinking into the soft cushions at the back, and an overwhelming sense of lassitude swept over him, so that he was content merely to lie back and ask no further questions until the girl had slipped in behind the wheel and they were moving off.

Sitting as straight as possible in his seat, he threw a quick glance behind him as they drove away. Down below, a column of smoke was still lifting into the clear air, a column that was shredded and blown into oblivion by the wind sighing up the steep slope of the mountain. There was now only the vaguest hint of flame among the rocks.

Francesca drove fast, taking the bends at speed. Evidently she knew the stretch of road like the back of her hand, he reflected weakly. Licking his dry lips, he said harshly: 'How did you know it was me down there, Francesca?'

'It's quite simple, really. I heard that you had arrived in Sofia and guessed that you might be trying to contact Volescu. That was one of his men driving the car. I also discovered that someone is keeping a watch on your room at the hotel. That was when I decided to follow you. I had Carl come with me just in case you ran into any trouble on the way. By the time we saw that other car, it was too late. Both you and they had too good a lead on us. We saw most of what happened, saw you go over the edge. It was then a toss-up whether we went after them or went to help you.'

'I'm glad you reached the right decision as far as my particular welfare was concerned,' he said, trying to keep evenness in his tone.

'We can always find the others when we need to,' said Carl thickly. He spoke in halting English.

The girl nodded. 'Carl is right. We know where to find them.'

Just around a bend, they ran through a small town, which Carradine guessed was Zlatica. When they were through and out into the open country once more, he said: 'But you still haven't explained how you came to be here — in Bulgaria. The last I saw of you, you were being taken away from Tamariu in that motor launch. I thought that would be the last I'd ever see of you.'

Through the rear mirror, he saw the faint smile on Francesca's lips. She pressed gently on the accelerator with her foot, bringing the needle on the speedometer up to the hundred kilometre mark. 'There was a little unpleasantness in Tamariu, I must admit. But nothing that we were unable to take care of.'

'It was the fat man behind it all, wasn't it?'

She nodded briefly. 'He played right into our hands,' she said confidently. 'He was an amateur when it comes to that sort of work.'

'Oh?' Carradine smiled again. 'Meaning by that, you are a professional.'

'More so than he and his thugs turned out to be,' she told him crisply. 'It seems that you and I are in the same kind of business.'

Carradine narrowed his eyes and sharpened his mind at that remark. 'I'm afraid I don't understand,' he said slowly.

'No?' She laughed, a pleasant sound. 'We at the Deuxieme Bureau are also very interested in Professor Ubyenkov and his discovery. I have been ordered to give you all the assistance I can. Naturally, I am hoping to find him before you do, but — '

'I see. For the honour of France, of course.'

'Naturellement.' She tossed her head, blonde curls shaking and dancing from side to side, shining in the sunlight that slanted in through the windscreen. 'Volescu is waiting for you at Kazanluk, I believe.'

'That's right.'

'Then I shall take you there. Perhaps he can help you, perhaps not. I have my own leads to follow.'

'And naturally, you don't intend to tell me what they are at the moment.'

'If we find Ubyenkov, then I shall let you know.'

Carradine nodded, sank back into his seat, relaxing. This was a turn of events that he had not anticipated, yes he had to admit that the girl had shown up at the most opportune time as far as he was concerned. He had had the feeling when he had first met her in Tamariu that she was onto something that went deeper than just political intrigue. He had the greatest respect for the members of the Deuxieme Bureau. He had worked with them on several occasions and in spite of the friendly rivalry that existed between the two organisations, they both knew they were fighting for the same cause.

They passed through Karlovo and Shipka and drove along the winding mountain road to Kazanluk. Nowhere along the road did they see any sign of the red car. There were many places where it could have turned off the road, the men inside it, confident that they had performed the task well, that he and the driver were both dead and they had nothing more to fear from either of them.

A little after three o'clock in the afternoon, they drove into Kazanluk, with the tall mountains looming high in the distance. The girl stopped the car close to the kerb and left it in gear with her foot on the clutch.

'Anton Volescu lives in that house at the corner of the street,' she said, pointing.

'Aren't you coming?' Carrington asked in surprise as he opened the door.

She shook her head. 'Whatever he can tell you, I feel that Carl and I already know. But I'm sure that we shall meet again, soon.'

Getting out of the car, conscious of his dishevelled appearance and the blood on his forehead where it had flowed from the deep cut, he lifted his hand in salute and stepped back as she let in the clutch. The car roared off into the distance, through the main street, and vanished a few moments later.

Slowly, he made his way towards the house that Francesca had pointed out to him. There were a few people on the streets and he was vaguely glad of this. The house looked deserted as he came up to it. He noticed that it sat by itself, away from the others, separated by two narrow alleys that twisted away from the square. Giving a quick glance up and down the street, Carradine knocked loudly on the door. It was opened a few moments later by a tall, bull-necked man with a mop of flaming red hair. Bulgarian? thought

Carradine, with red hair?

'Anton Volescu?' Carradine asked. He spoke in French.

The other nodded, then motioned him inside. The door closed behind them.

4

THE MAN WITH THE SPARKLING SECRET

Carradine followed the tall man in silence, along two passages that ran deeper into the building, then into a long, wide room fitted out more luxuriously than he would ever have guessed from the outside appearance of the building. Volescu motioned him to a chair, sat down in the other near the small desk, crossed his legs, then pushed a large box of cigarettes over to him. He did not speak until they were both smoking.

'From the obvious fact that you arrived here alone, I gather that something has happened to Zdenko, my chauffeur?' The thick, bushy brows lifted a little in interrogation.

Carradine nodded his head slowly. The sweet-tasting tobacco of the cigarette, which was so obviously Turkish, was

111

something he had not enjoyed for several years. 'We were followed from Sofia. I noticed someone watching my room at the hotel when I woke and your man was some minutes late arriving, although he had impressed on me that punctuality was vital. Anyway, they shot us up on the road here. Your driver was killed. Whether it was from a bullet or from the crash when we went over the edge, I'm not sure, though he had at least six slugs in him.'

'So that is where you received that cut,' murmured the other, a faint note of sympathy in his deep voice. 'I will arrange for someone to see to it for you, but first, if you feel up to it, there are some questions I must ask. You know how things are here. The Reds are watching everything, even here in Kazanluk. In Sofia, of course, it is even worse. They know of everyone who comes into the country. Hotel staff, the secret police, have all been bribed to pass on this information.' He smiled warmly. 'We, of course, do the same so there is little to be gained on either side.'

'But everyone has to be sure that nothing gets past them.'

'Exactly. I see that you understand these matters perfectly. But — ' He let his severe, powerful gaze rest on Carradine for a long moment and then spoke through the blue haze of cigarette smoke, ' — if the car went over the edge, how did you manage to get here?'

'Fortunately, I was seen by one of my more recent acquaintances and she gave me a lift into Kazanluk.'

Volescu's eyebrows almost vanished into the thick mop of red hair. 'A woman in the game,' he said easily, but there was a clear detectable look of surprise and suspicion in his voice. 'You'll forgive me, my friend, but I have long since made it a rule to be extremely careful. I find that one tends to live a little longer that way. This woman, you know her?'

Carradine gave a quick nod. 'You've no need to worry. She's working for the Deuxieme Bureau.'

Volescu's eyes narrowed just a shade. 'And is she looking for Professor Ubyenkov also?'

'Yes.' It was clear that he must keep nothing back from this man if he was to get the help he needed.

'I see.' Volescu sat back and smoked a cigarette without speaking, his eyes lost in thought. 'There have been many little things happening during the past few weeks, things which I do not fully understand and which puzzle and frighten me a little. I can smell trouble, big trouble. But for men such as us, that is nothing to run away from. Trouble is the — how do you say it? — spice of life for us.'

'I agree.' Carradine hesitated, then went on slowly: 'Do you have any doubts about this girl? Her name is Francesca Romano — at least that was the name she went by when we first met.'

'It could be her real name, of course,' said Volescu. He stubbed out his cigarette in the silver tray. 'The fact that she is here means one of two things. Either she is, as she claims to be, working for the French Government on this case — or she is working for the enemy camp. Whichever it is, I suggest we treat her with the utmost caution until we know for certain. I will do my best to find out.'

Carradine sat back. There was a faint note of tension in his voice as he said: 'There is one thing which may have a bearing on this. I met her in Tamariu on the Spanish coast before I was assigned to this mission. There was a man following her there. The last I saw of her, she was being taken away by him, and some other thugs, in a speedboat. When I questioned her about this, she said that he was just an amateur and that he had played into their hands when he had abducted her. If it's possible, I'd like to know who that man is.'

'Or was,' smiled Volescu. 'From what you have just said, he may no longer be alive.' He uttered a harsh, barking laugh. 'But at least you are here, my friend. Now we must discuss what you have to do. Naturally, I will give you all of the information I have.' His eyes had suddenly hardened, growing dark and shrewd. 'We know that Ubyenkov came into Bulgaria across the Romanian frontier nine days ago. I know nothing of what he has to sell or why he is suddenly so important to London.' His smile grew crafty. 'It must be of vital importance, however, for them to send you here. I have heard of you, by reputation, of course.'

Tightly, Carradine said: 'So far as I'm concerned, there is only one thing I need to know. The exact whereabouts of Ubyenkov.'

'That, I'm afraid, is something I do not know. All I can tell you is that he is somewhere near Balchik. My local head-quarters there reported that he had been seen on two occasions in the centre. Will that help you?'

Carradine gave a tight-lipped nod. It was as much as he could expect. After all, if the Reds could not find him, it stood to reason that the man had gone to earth and concealed his burrow very cleverly. Considering that his life would be forfeit if the Reds caught him, it was only reasonable that he should have taken every possible precaution to hide himself until he felt sure that anyone looking for him came from the West. Even then, it might be difficult trying to persuade him of his true identity, Carradine reflected. But that was a bridge he would have to cross when he came to it. Sufficient for the moment was the fact that he had a rough idea where he was.

'Can you get me to Balchik?'

'Nothing could be easier, my friend. But you do not have to leave right away. Tomorrow will be time enough to get you there. One thing I will be able to find out — if any Red agent gets to him first. So far, there is no indication of that.' He went on seriously: 'But I must now arrange for a doctor to attend to your injuries. From what you tell me, you are very fortunate to be still alive. Evidently those two men did not intend you to reach me.'

'Obviously.' Carradine found himself warming to the other. There was something about this man, some positive thinking, a direct outlook, that of a man who faced everything but the completely impossible with a definite will to win.

The doctor was a small, thin-faced man. He looked to be of peasant stock, but Carradine was forced to grudgingly acknowledge that he knew his job; unlike several of the Eastern European doctors he had met. Half an hour after arriving in Kazanluk, Carradine was seated in a room at the rear of the large building on the corner of the square. He had to admit that Volescu did himself proud when it came to accommodation. The room might have been faithfully copied from a picture of one of the suites at the Dorchester in London, or the Istanbul-Hilton situated on the heights of Pera, both of which he had frequented on various occasions.

The Bulgarian doctor had covered the cut in his forehead with a collodion solution when Carradine had refused a bandage. It had stung at first, but now, eyeing himself in the full-length crystal mirror, he was forced to admit that it performed its function satisfactorily and did not show except on close inspection. There had been a momentary sense of disappointment when Volescu had informed him that he did not know the exact where-abouts of Ubyenkov, but that was gone now and already his mind was working, thinking ahead in an effort to assess all of the possibilities and probabilities.

Now he racked his brain for a way of getting close to Ubyenkov without scaring the other. The man would be afraid, and a frightened man acted in strange ways, especially when he could not be sure who were his friends, or who his enemies might be. As soon as one man got in contact with him, he would have to be one hundred percent certain that the man was who he said he was. Ubyenkov, although unused to the ways of espionage and counter-espionage, would have heard of double agents, would know that he could not even afford to make that single, first mistake, which other men might be allowed to make — and live.

Sitting back in his chair by the window, Carradine lit one of the Turkish cigars which Volescu had insisted on giving him, claiming — and no doubt rightly — that the Western democracies did not know how to grow, or process, tobacco. He drew the sweet-tasting smoke down into his lungs and forced himself to relax, but it was only his body that he could relax;

his brain kept on working overtime, coming up with various ideas, only to reject them almost at once. The fact that he had almost been killed that very morning, told him the nature of the opposition here, men who would stick at nothing. For the first time since he had left England, he was beginning to feel glad that he had accepted those weapons which Forbes had thrust on him.

He spent the rest of that evening with Volescu and two of his men, discussing every piece of evidence they had as to the whereabouts of Ubyenkov and what the other's most probable movements would be once he arrived in Bulgaria. At the end of four hours, with the air in the room full of blue cigarette smoke and empty cups in front of them, they were still no nearer the solution than when they had started. It was up to Carradine to locate him and then try to get him — or his secret — out of the country and back to the West. Volescu would put all of his resources at Carradine's disposal once that was done, and offered to make things go a little more smoothly than usual in getting out

120

of the country. Carradine was soon brought to the realisation that, as well as being one of the Chief's most trusted agents in Bulgaria, the other had contacts inside the Government there and in most of the Governmental departments. No doubt the enemy possessed similar facilities, but this did not detract from the usefulness of what Volescu could do, and Carradine realised that.

'One of my men will drive you to Balchik early tomorrow morning. After the regrettable incident today, you will both be on your guard.' As he spoke, he nodded towards a big, broad-shouldered man seated at the table next to Carradine. 'Kaltek here knows what to do in case of any trouble.'

'Good.' Carradine rubbed a hand over his chin thoughtfully. 'What kind of place is Balchik?'

The other pursed his lips. 'About the same size as Kazanluk. It's on the coast, of course, and it may be that this is the way Ubyenkov used to get there, rather than overland through Romania.'

'It would certainly have been easier for

him, more able to avoid detection.'

'When will we reach there?'

'In a fast car, a little after midday. There is a man called Nerim in Balchik. He manages my local headquarters. A good man but stupid in one way. He prefers to use a knife rather than his brain. He uses it to such good advantage that there have been several occasions when I have been forced to reprimand him. Unless he learns to control his temper, it means that we shall lose more of the enemy agents I would like to have alive — at least, until there has been a chance to get them to talk.'

Carradine said nothing. He noticed the way in which the other's dark, glittering eyes had suddenly gone opaque, and he knew how Volescu would get the information he needed from such men as were unfortunate enough to fall into his hands alive.

★　★　★

The low-bonneted car sped swiftly through the streets of Kazanluk just as the dawn was breaking in the east, a greying dawn which swiftly flamed to a brilliant red. The clouds that hung low on the horizon where the undulating mountains formed sharp, ragged upthrusts of black shadow, lost their flat, cardboard appearance and filled out, becoming three-dimensional. The sun rose when they were thirty kilometres from Kazanluk, heading northeast. The mean twisting streets on the outskirts of the town were left behind now and they were out in the clean, pure air of the mountains. There was little traffic on the roads and Kaltek kept his foot firmly depressed on the accelerator. The dark, brooding forests occasionally pulled themselves down the slopes, closing in on both sides of the road and watching them through the window of the speeding car, Carradine had the feeling that the tales which were told of the Hertz mountains in Germany applied equally well here. This was a country where, with the night, black horror came creeping out of the shadows; a legend-haunted place of ancient ruined castles and a blood-stained history that went back over the long centuries. His instinct told him, as no doubt it must have told countless other travellers, that this was a place from which he would be lucky to get out alive.

They drove on from the mountains, through Kornobat and Aitos, then turned north towards Cliflik. By eleven-fifteen, they were slowing down for the drive through Stalin, characteristically changed by the new regime from the original name of Varna. Somehow, Carradine thought he liked the old name better; and from Kaltek he learned that most of the older inhabitants of the town called it by that name, refusing to recognise the change. Discreetly, of course. To have done so openly would have been asking for trouble. They now took the coast road, which finally deposited them at Balchik.

Carradine looked about him with interest as Kaltek drove along a narrow cobbled street that led off from the main through road. This was apparently all part of the town. Far below, he could just glimpse the reflected light of the high noon sun off the waters of the sea. That would be the Black Sea, he thought to himself, with Sevastopol due east. Now he was very close to Russia.

The car stopped. Turning his head, breaking himself out of his reverie, he glanced about it. They were outside a bowl-roofed building which, from the outside, reminded Carradine of a warehouse. From the inside, he saw that this was exactly what it was. Kaltek led him over the creaking wooden boards of the wide floor to a door set in the wall at the far end. There were huge crates stacked high along one wall. Black market? Or a legitimate business carried on as a front to the sort of work this man really did?

Kaltek led him through the door into a large office, glass-fronted so that the man who rose to his feet behind the desk was able to look down into the entire building.

The other came around the side of the desk and took Carradine's hand in a firm grip. He seemed to sense Carradine's thoughts for he said with a faint smile: 'Anton has perhaps given you a picture of what we are doing here. No doubt he has told you that we do nothing.'

'Not exactly, but — '

Nerim laughed harshly. 'You do not have to be embarrassed, my friend. I know Anton Volescu and he knows me. He gives the orders from the office in Kazanluk and I carry them out to the best of my ability. He says that my one failing is the work I do with this — ' He moved his right hand with a deceptive slowness. When it came back into sight, the bright light streaming through a skylight in the ceiling glinted bluely off the long, double-edged blade of the throwing knife he held.

Carradine let his gaze stray down to the weapon, then looked up into the other's face and gave a faint nod.

Nerim returned the nod, then thrust the knife back somewhere into the folds of his baggy trousers. 'That is as I thought. However, for once he is wrong. My men have been keeping a close watch on the old castle just north of the town, overlooking the bay. There has been some activity going on there for a little while now. Lights seen at night. Naturally the townspeople will not go there. They are a superstitious lot. But I — I do not believe in these old tales. I say to myself, Nerim, why should there be light showing there unless because someone is up there, someone who does not want to be disturbed in what he is doing?'

'And what have you found out?' For some unknown reason, Carradine felt a stir of exhilaration.

'I think that is where they have hidden Professor Ubyenkov. He is the man you seek — no?'

'Yes. If that is where he is, then you must be able to contact them, whoever they are who are hiding him, get word to them who I am and why I'm here.'

Nerim shrugged. 'It's not as easy as that, I'm afraid. They will be wary and suspicious of everyone. They know what will happen to all of them, not just to this one man, if the Soviets get there first. They cannot be sure of me, or of you.'

'Then what do you suggest I do? You have had experience of the country around here. You must know a way of getting there without being seen.'

'It may be possible. They will be watching. But the two others may get through any guards they have. If only we knew who these people are who are helping him.'

'When can we go?' Quite suddenly, Carradine was anxious to have this over with, to waste no more time. He already knew that the Soviet agents responsible for Ubyenkov were playing for keeps and the sooner they got him out of the country, the better.

'Tonight. I will come with you. This is an operation that calls for a great deal of care and ingenuity. I know that old ruin from my boyhood. I can find my way through the underground cellars and the long passages which few people dream exist.'

This was far better than Carradine had ever expected. If Nerim knew that castle there on the hill as well as he claimed, they should have little difficulty in slipping past any guards, in getting to the men who were keeping Ubyenkov hidden. Once they got that close, they ought to be able to convince these men that they were

128

friends, that all they wanted was to get the professor out of Eastern Europe and back to London.

'In the meantime, you will stay here,' went on the other soberly. 'The fewer people in Balchik who know that you are here, the better. We will leave as soon after dark as is possible.'

★   ★   ★

Slowly, Carradine moved through the narrow alley filled with piles of stinking refuse, the high walls of the building outside bearing down on them, dark and featureless. There were a few windows that were unbroken but for the most part there were only ragged slivers of glass in them, sticking into the old mortar, reflecting the pale yellow light of the moon, which was little more than a scratch of light low in the west.

'There aren't many people abroad in this part of the town after dark,' Nerim said. 'If there are, they mostly know me and move on without asking any awkward questions.'

They walked on down the alley, slipping across a patch of pale moonlight and a small square where yellow lights showed in several of the windows, all the time working their way north until they reached the outskirts of Balchik.

Here, Nerim inched his way forward, picking his way over the huge cobbles which formed at the surface of the alley. There were long shadows here and in spite of the tight grip he had on himself, Carradine imagined that there were men in those shadows and unfriendly eyes watching their every move, biding their time to strike.

About a hundred metres from the spot where the narrow road wound out of the town and up into the craggy hills overlooking the bay, Carradine suddenly paused. Pulling Nerim into the shadows, he motioned the other to remain quiet. A tram clanked its way up the hill in the distance, rumbled into view for a few seconds across the far end of the alley along which they had worked their way, then vanished. The sound faded slowly.

Nerim cautiously turned his head and

looked round at Carradine. 'What is it?' he asked in a soft whisper.

'There's someone following us,' Carradine said tautly, his voice reaching the other and no further. 'There he comes.'

Nerim let his breath go in a soft hiss close to Carradine's ear. One of the shadows fifty metres away had suddenly moved. A man materialised out of the gaping mouth of one of the narrow intersecting alleys, hung poised on his feet for a moment, then darted noiselessly along the wall of a building that fronted the square.

Carradine had caught only a brief glimpse of the other as he darted across that open space, but it had been enough for him to recognise who it was. His grip on Nerim's arm tightened convulsively.

'You know him?' murmured the other. It was more a statement than a question.

'I met up with him for a brief period in Tamariu, in Spain,' Carradine said tonelessly. 'He's a Red agent. I'm sure of it.'

'Then we must take care of him,' murmured Nerim. 'In this business we cannot afford to take chances.' He reached down and withdrew the long-bladed knife from his belt. Padding forward, he kept close to the wall, a wraith-like shadow just visible to Carradine. The other waited for a moment, then followed him. His instinct told him that the Red spider would stand no chance against the knife, though inwardly he felt a faint sense of revulsion at the idea of killing a man in cold blood as Nerim was about to do. He had killed men himself in the past, but always the other had had an even chance of defending himself.

The fat man was coming forward out of the shadow now, still unaware that he had been seen, that death was on its way to him. Less than forty metres away, he stepped momentarily to the edge of the narrow pavement, body bent forward lightly. There was something in his right fist and in that same instant, he saw Nerim and brought up his arm. There was a savage spurt of orange flame from the gun in his hand, the faint pop of the silencer, and the leaden smack of the bullet striking the wall as Nerim flung himself sideways. Even as he went down, the Bulgarian drew back his hand and flung the knife in a glittering arc through the air.

There was a tinkle of metal hitting the wall. Then the dark shadow of the fat man moved, back to the alley from where he had appeared. The hollow clatter of his feet on the cobbles faded swiftly as he ran. Jumping Nerim's sprawling body, Carradine ran to the end of the alley, his Luger in his fists. In front of him, the alley stretched away like a river of midnight, but there was no sign of the man. Reluctantly, he went back to Nerim and helped him to his feet.

'Are you hurt?' Carradine asked tightly. He felt an edge of anger blur his voice, anger at the fact that the fat man had got away.

Nerim smiled grimly, tight-faced. He brushed the dirt off his clothes with his hands, then went forward and picked up his knife from where it lay on the pavement, examined it carefully, then slid it back into his belt. 'I'm all right, my friend. I thought I had him, but he was too quick for me. I suppose he's gone?'

'He could be a kilometre away by now,' Carradine affirmed. 'We have no chance of catching him now, even if we had the time. But I doubt if we'll be troubled by him tonight.'

'You're right,' agreed the other. 'It's a pity, but we cannot wait and waste time looking for him. Let us go on to the castle.'

They left the town and took the winding path that led up the steep, rocky slope. The waters of the Black Sea glimmered faintly in the pale moonlight. Over their heads, the stars were out in their thousands, swarming across the dark velvet of the sky. Carradine moved up the slope as quickly as his feet would carry him, stumbling occasionally where a moon-thrown shadow hid a treacherous rock.

'Slowly, my friend,' said Nerim quietly. 'To hurry now could be fatal.'

With an effort, Carradine forced himself to move more cautiously. In the moonlight, he could just make out the tall, sky-rearing ruins of the castle, perched like some antediluvian monster on top of the high crags. On one side of it, the ground plummeted away in a sheer precipitous slope so that the castle appeared to be hanging eternally on the edge of the abyss, needing only a faint puff of wind to send it dropping down into the soft swell of the Black Sea.

They came on the shallow, worn stone steps five minutes later and Nerim motioned Carradine up them, bringing up the rear. Halfway up, there was a glimmering of water and they splashed across a swift-running stream that ran down the mountainside. In the moon-light, it was difficult to make out which were shadows and which were razor-edged gullies, where a man could snap his ankle like a rotten twig if he put a foot wrong.

Suddenly, Nerim was beside him, breathing heavily from the exertion, and his eyes glittering brightly in his head, his teeth just showing as a faint gleam in his shadowed face. 'It is quite a long climb. There is, of course, a track which goes all the way up, but that is the way they will watch. Very few know of this way into the castle. I discovered it myself when I was only a small child and since then I have prided myself that no one else knows of it. But we must be careful now. The rocks and stones are slippery with moss and very treacherous. One slip and you will go over the side and down into the sea.'

Carradine threw a quick glance downward, then immediately looked up again. He had not realised they were so close to the edge now, and they had somehow wound around in a spiral, the narrow track twisting outward until it came around a broad outcrop of stone almost directly beneath the castle ruins. When Nerim had said that no one bothered to watch this way up, he could see why the other had been so sure. Only a fool would attempt this climb in broad daylight. At night, with only a faint flooding of yellow moonlight, it was almost suicidal.

The sheer steepness of the slope now was frightening. It took a great deal of concentration not to look down. A loose stone rattling down from the rocks started

Carradine's heart thumping in his chest, hammering against his ribs until it felt as though it must surely burst. Very slowly, a metre at a time, they climbed up the slope. It was a climb such as Carradine had never made before, such as he knew he could never make again. This was insane, he told himself fiercely. There had to be a better and easier way up than this. Good God, they were climbing the sheer wall of the cliff, while below them, almost directly beneath, the breakers were hammering on the jagged teeth of the black rocks that glistened wetly in the moonlight.

A few metres away to his right, Nerim went up hand over hand, finding handholds and toeholds where none seemed to exist, hauling himself now over the smoothly swelling convexity of an overhang, edging along a narrow ledge that could barely be seen. They reached a wider portion of a ledge and Nerim wormed his way over to where Carradine sat, with his back to the smooth rocks, the palms of his hands pressed tightly against it on either side of his body, his feet dangling over the edge in empty space. He felt anything but secure or comfortable.

'Not much further to go now, my friend. Perhaps fifty metres. Then there is an easy stretch before we move into the castle.' He grinned, as though the whole affair was one huge joke, something to be savoured and enjoyed.

Carradine looked up at the stretch above him speculatively, and nodded in silence. He wiped his sweating forehead. There was no time for any more.

Nerim began to work his way cautiously along the ledge. Above them, the looming, tessellated walls of the great castle lifted in the moonlight, towering more than a hundred feet into the clear air. The ledge was narrow, not more than three metres wide at its broadest, tapering off into the gloom on either side. Worse still, a little later it seemed to vanish altogether and Nerim's shadowy figure had disappeared around a sharply outthrusting impassable barrier.

Back to this wall of rock, Carradine was forced to stand on his heels, his hands outspread, the palms inward against the cliff, pressing in to it in order to maintain his precarious balance. But in less than two minutes he had somehow managed to follow the other around, out to where the rock sloped upwards, angling a little to the right. He felt bitterly cold now and there was a stiff breeze blowing in off the Black Sea, and the sharp edges of the rocks bit cruelly into the calves of his legs and his hands. The climb had been a nightmare, more difficult and exhausting than he had expected, looking up at it from below. But the moonlight had been deceiving. It had tended to smooth out the contours, to make them seem smoother than they actually were.

Deliberately, he forced his mind away from the aches and pains in his limbs, from his body's insistent demands for rest. Somehow, Nerim was moving up and he knew that he must follow. His shoulder muscles were afire with agony by the time he reached the top and felt Nerim's hands come down, grip his wrists tightly and pull steadily, easing him over the top where the crumbling earth crushed and broke under him. His breath rasped in great gulping inhalations into his heaving lungs and for an interminable moment, he seemed to be hanging by his fingertips over the lip of the cliff. Then, slowly, he moved out on to the broad stretch of open ground and lay quite still, forcing feeling and life back into his bruised body.

Nerim waited patiently until he sat up, then said in a soft whisper: 'Are you ready to go on?'

He nodded and swallowed thickly. 'Let's go,' he said harshly. Straightening his legs, he hoisted himself forward off the ground, arm straight, palms still on the dirt in front of him, his head lifted. Then he stopped and hissed a faint warning to the other; but it had not been needed. Nerim, too, had seen the shadow that had moved suddenly. Thirty, maybe forty metres away, close to the edge of the tall ruins, the dark shape slowly straightened and detached itself from the wealth of dark shadows that grew beneath them castle walls. It was advancing slowly in their direction.

There could be no mistake now. Tall and square, it was a man — a guard in all probability, for there could have been no one else at this time of the night — and because of this castle's reputation the other would undoubtedly be doubly cautious. For the first two or three seconds, the two men lay absolutely motionless. The other had not seen them, but he was suspicious, his head turning this way and that into the thinly keening wind, striving to catch again the faint sounds that had obviously attracted his attention.

But now that the first shock of discovery was over, Carradine's mind was working clearly again. To go on now would be suicidal. The faintest movement would be instantly seen by the other. At night, as Carradine well knew, averted vision was by far the more acute and the sentry might catch any sudden movement out of the corner of his eye.

If that happened, the other would only have to turn his head and it would be the end. Even in the darkness, with only a faint trace of moonlight now touching the top of the cliffs, their silhouettes would be easily discernible against the skyline.

Bending his head, he whispered to Nerim: 'Stay here, wait until I get into the rocks and then try to cause a diversion.'

'What are you going to do?' murmured the other. There was a flash of white teeth in his shadowed features. 'Perhaps with my knife I may — '

'No! Too far.' Carradine shook his head slightly. 'Besides, you'd have to get to your feet to throw it with any chance of hitting him.'

For a moment, he thought the other intended to argue, then the other nodded. Gradually, every movement as smooth and controlled as possible, his breath easing in and out of his lungs, Carradine slithered forward over the rough, uneven ground. Still the shadowy figure was advancing, making for a point very close to the rocks where Carradine meant to be. Another twenty-five metres to go. Even as he crawled forward, Carradine knew that he could never make it in time. The other was moving too quickly now. Then, sharp against the wind, came the sound of something striking rock over to his left. Out of the corner of his vision, he saw the man whirl abruptly, head twisting round, peering off into the rocks near the base of the castle wall. Nerim must have seen the danger and thrown a stone into the rocks to distract the other's attention. When the man's back was turned, Carradine thrust himself forward with a powerful heave of his legs, then wriggled out of sight among the jumble of boulders that lay strewn in front of him. By the time the man in the greatcoat had turned, evidently convinced that it had been nothing more than a loose stone falling from above, Carradine was well out of sight in the rocks.

In the pale shaft of yellow moonlight, he caught a glimpse of the face under the soft hat; an off-white, straining face. Clearly the man had no liking for his task here. Carradine remembered some of the tales which were rife in this part of the world concerning these old, and ruined castles and knew that if the other was as superstitious as the vast majority of the folk here, then the thoughts that would be running through his mind at that moment were far from wholesome ones. Every faint sound would bring a brief wash of terror to his mind.

The setting moon, just visible, was now throwing a sickly glow over everything. The wild rocks looked down on the rolling waters of the Black Sea; and above all, dominating the scene, was the old castle, legend-haunted, filled with the ghosts and the black terror that was enshrined in this place. Slowly, gauging his time and distance, Carradine waited. The man came on, made to move past his hiding place, then stopped in mid-stride as Nerim uttered a low whistle. Instantly, the other spun, turning his back to Carradine.

For a moment the man stood stock still, clearly trying to estimate the origin of the sound. Then his hand moved into the pocket of the coat and brought out a snub-nosed automatic, the metal glinting in the faint light. He had taken only a single step forward when Carradine moved, cat-footed, out of the rocks. The other seemed to have a brief flash of insight, but the warning that someone was behind him had barely reached his brain; he had only just begun to turn, when Carradine was on him. There was a sudden explosive gasp from the man as Carradine's boot hit him just behind the right knee. Before he could utter a further sound, the straight edge of Carradine's hand hit him just behind the ear. It was not a killing blow, delivered with just the right amount of force to knock the other unconscious. He would be out for some hours now.

Quickly he stopped, hooked his hands under the other's armpits, straightened, and hauled him out of sight among the rocks. Soon, perhaps, some of his companions might start looking for him and it was essential that he should not be found too soon.

'Is he dead?' Nerim asked dispassionately.

'No.' Carradine shook his head, staring down at the unconscious man. 'He's probably fighting for the same thing as we are. If he's one of the men helping Ubyenkov then there is no reason to kill him.' It was part of Carradine's work to kill people, but he was always glad when there was no real necessity to kill. This man would come round in a few hours with nothing worse than a sore neck.

The darkly shadowed ruins swallowed them up a few moments later. Nerim led the way more quickly now. It was obvious from his movements that he knew every twist and turn in these passages which had been hewn out of the solid stone beneath the castle. Reaching the end of one of them, he paused and crouched down on his knees, motioning Carradine to do likewise.

'This passage leads up through the old dungeons into the castle proper,' he whispered, his words rustling back at them in an eerie echo from the damp, moss-covered walls. 'They must have him hidden down here. It would be too open up there and — '

'Quiet!' hissed Carradine. The rustling silence crowded down on them from every side. Across the passage, there was a skittering sound. Something large and grey and furry came out into the open and perched on top of a fallen stone. Red eyes glared at them from the shadows. A bewhiskered face, narrowed to the snout, appeared in their direction. Then there was another. Carradine felt the muscles of his stomach tighten as the rats came out of their holes and crouched, poised in a wide semi-circle.

'These must have been what you heard,' said Nerim softly. He uttered a sharp bark of a laugh. 'This place is running with those little grey creatures. They resent our intrusion here.'

Carradine sucked in his breath sharply. Ugly little bastards, he thought to himself. He could visualise them crawling over his body. Memories of Edgar Allan Poe crept into his mind and it was impossible for him to thrust them away. This was just the sort of setting he would have relished. Lord Dunsany, Lovecraft — all of them would have been quite at home here.

Getting to their feet, they walked along the echo-ringing passage, the looming walls broken here and there. Large drops of cold water fell on their heads from the curving roof. There was very little light and for the most part they were forced to find their way forward by touch.

Now the wide passage was coming to an end. Carradine felt the moss-covered wall move away from him beneath his trailing hand. He heard Nerim fiddling behind him.

'We're just moving through into the dungeons,' whispered Nerim. 'Watch your feet. There are still several of the old instruments of torture left here.'

Carradine nodded in the darkness. He kept his mouth closed and breathed slowly and easily through his nostrils. If only there was some light so that he could see what he was doing.

Scarcely had the thought crossed his mind than a glare of light burst into incandescent brilliance all about them. For a long second, he felt utterly paralysed. His eyes were dazzled by the light. He could see nothing that moved or went on beyond that fiery, eye-searing glare. And it was, literally, eye-searing, for there seemed to be heat at the back of it too.

Instinctively, his right hand dropped for the gun. His fingers closed on the smooth metal of the butt and he tried to drag it clear of the cloth of his pocket.

Beside him, he discerned Nerim moving forward, going down into an instinctive crouch, the glitter of the knife in his hand. Vaguely, he was aware of movement, of wavering shadows that appeared through the bright glare as his pupils contracted painfully. His reaction was automatic. There was very little reason behind it. The shock of what had happened had robbed him of that. He took one quick step forward, finger tightening on the trigger. Then the whole castle seemed to fall in on him as something hit him hard on the back of the head.

5

THE FOURTH DEGREE

The harsh light, glaring redly even through closed lids, brought Steve Carradine back to consciousness. He did not move. Keeping his body completely still, he waited while all of his senses came alert like those of an animal. Eyes closed, forcing the lids to remain motionless, knowing that if he was being watched, this would give him away at once, he listened to the noises that went on around him. There was a vague murmur of conversation off in the distance, a sound like a beetle drone that faded and then approached in an oddly disturbing manner, although he guessed that this was due to his physical condition more than to anything else.

He forced himself to recall the events that led up to him being there. He remembered moving along that stone passage with Nerim close beside him. Then that glaring light which seemed to have come from nowhere and his being hit on the back of the head. After that, there was nothing.

A bolt of water, icy-cold, struck him in the face. Coughing and retching, he tried to move now, but found that his arms were anchored tightly behind his back. Slowly, his eyes and brain cleared. The musty, decaying smell of the deep dungeon hit him forcibly; yet the harsh, glaring light was oddly out of place in this world of dim shadowed walls and age-old antiquity.

A voice, flat, uninterested, coldly ominous, said from the back of the harsh, actinic light: 'Now you will tell me the truth. Who are you? Who sent you here? How much do you know?'

With an effort, he forced his eyes to take in what lay behind the glare. He saw the indistinct shape that sat a few metres away, and blinked his eyes as the water ran into them from the hair plastered over his forehead. Straining the muscles of his neck, he lifted his head. The quick look around him made the throbbing at the back of his temples hurt even worse than before. Dimly, he made out the shapes of various implements about him, of light shining off rusted metal and twisted leather straps.

'Do you think you could turn that light in the other direction?' he said, forcing evenness into his tone. 'I don't think too well with it glaring into my eyes.'

'Ah, how inconsiderate of me.' The light suddenly swung away from Carradine's face and he was able to make out details more clearly now. The man who sat in the chair a short distance away was short and stubby, a large moon face set above a thick-set neck. He sat bolt upright as though on a judge's bench addressing some felon in the dock, and there was a faintly mocking smile on his thick, rubbery lips.

'Thank you.' Experimentally, Carradine felt the bonds that tied him to the chair. They had been pulled tight, giving him no play at all, the knot evidently having been made by an expert.

'Now, to get back to the all-important

point,' went on the other smoothly. 'I know a great deal about you, why you came to Balchik. But there are one or two things I do not know, but I am certain that you will provide me the answers very soon.'

Carradine thought fast. There was the scent of danger in his nostrils, something he had learned to recognise. He squeezed his eyes tightly together, then open them again. 'If you know so much about me,' he said quietly, 'then I suggest you know enough. I don't intend to tell you anything until I know what is going on around here.'

'I rather fear that you are in no position to temporise,' said the other softly. He spoke in a quiet, conversational tone, yet there was an undercurrent of danger audible in it. 'We also have your companion. He may not know as much as you, but I think that if I were to allow my — associates — to work on him in your presence, you might be persuaded to talk. If not, then we have our own ways of loosening stubborn tongues.'

'Just who are you?' Carradine asked.

'I should have thought that was obvious. Since there is no chance of your escape from here, I have no hesitation in telling you. One of my countrymen made a very big mistake. He decided to leave Russia, taking with him a very valuable secret, which he discovered while working for us, while taking the money we provided for his research. His ingratitude means little. But the fact that he intended to sell the secret to the West means a great deal. Naturally, this could not be allowed to happen.'

Very slowly, Carradine let his pent-up breath go in small pinches through his nostrils. He eyed the round, bland face of his interrogator closely. So they had been too late anyway. The Reds had got to Ubyenkov already. What had happened to him, and the men who had helped him, was anybody's guess. Carradine doubted if their end would have been swift and painless. Ubyenkov himself was possibly still alive. They would want to take him back to Russia where they could deal with him in their own inimical style.

'You express yourself most vividly,' he said.

'Naturally. I have the feeling that you are, perhaps, a British or American agent. We took into consideration the possibility that you would make an attempt to contact Ubyenkov once you learned of his disappearance from Russia. It was essential that we should forestall you.'

Out of the corner of his eye, Carradine saw the two men who stood behind the other's chair. The usual type of Soviet executioner, he thought grimly. Men who thought nothing of pain, particularly when it was someone else who was suffering it. Simple-minded men, more like animals than human beings, who obeyed orders blindly, without any question. Around the huge underground vault of stone, he could now make out the various contraptions that Nerim had spoken about; the old torture methods first originated in the Middle Ages, but were no less effective because of that. Many of them were just as efficient in loosening a man's tongue as the more subtle modern ways, scopolamine or hypnosis, or a dozen new drugs which obliterated a man's control over his mind and actions. He felt a little shiver run through him as he saw the wide, empty eyes fix themselves on his face. A trickle of sweat formed on his forehead and ran down into his eyes. The man would use the old ways first, he knew; if only because it would give him an added pleasure to see a fellow human being suffer.

How long could he hold out against this man? He wondered tensely. He tried again to loosen the thongs around his wrists, but felt them chafing into his flesh, and was forced to give up the attempt.

The sadistic eyes watched him for a moment with an almost amused expression. Then the other leaned forward a little in his chair. 'It is quite useless,' he murmured softly. 'Mischa is an expert at tying knots. But we are wasting time. Very soon, we shall be taking Professor Ubyenkov back to Russia, but first I want to know about you. I dislike leaving anything half-done. You have made things difficult for me already. One of my men died in the car which followed you from Sofia.'

'I'm glad to hear it,' Carradine said, forcing a smile. 'But I assure you that you are quite wrong about me. I was simply told in Balchik about the castle and decided to come and see it for myself. According to everything I was told, the place was deserted, and had been for more than two hundred years. The man who was with me acted as my guide. That's all.'

The other shook his head and said in a faintly bored voice: 'Please try to understand. No one tells Aleksandre Kreznikov that he has made a mistake. You underestimate me. I doubt if you have managed to find out anything at all about me. You have evidently been sent here to find Ubyenkov. He is here. I will tell you that because you will be totally unable to make any use of the fact. He is here in the castle, which, because of the ignorant superstition of the people living around Balchik, forms an excellent hideout for us until we leave, which will be very soon. It may be that they will find your body when we have left. But there are treacherous undercurrents in the Black Sea just below the castle and these have been known to drag down swimmers to the bottom and these poor, unfortunate men have never been seen again. The Black Sea appears to be particularly reluctant to give up her victims.'

Carradine sighed loudly. 'How often do I have to tell you that I don't know what you're talking about. Ask the man who was with me if you don't believe me.'

'Ah yes, Nerim. We know of him.' The way the other said it gave Carradine a little sinking feeling in his chest. He cursed himself inwardly for not realising that Kreznikov would have a file on all of Volescu's agents in Bulgaria. He closed his eyes again. His mind was whirring inside his head, coming up with ideas and instantly dismissing them. Somehow, he had to try to stall the other. Whatever happened, he must not give any hint of his reason for being there to Kreznikov. While he was still alive, while Nerim was alive — and the other had claimed he was — there was just a slender chance that an opportune moment might arise; and when it did, he must be in a better position to make the most of it. If only he had his hands free. There was a possibility that the other might consider the odds so tremendously weighted against him that he might agree to release his bonds. After all, with those two guards in this place, and God alone how many more scattered throughout the castle, he was taking scarcely any chance at all, letting him free.

He turned his head slowly towards the other. 'There seems to be this obsession in your mind that I'm a spy or something. Why can't you get it through that thick skull of yours that I'm not. If the man who led me here is known to you, that is no concern of mine. I merely asked for somebody who would guide me here.'

'Yet you came up the cliff, along the point where it is virtually unscalable and into the castle through the dungeons. Had your story been the truth, you would have come by the normal way, up the pass and in through the ruins. No, your story is a lie from start to finish. Evidently, too, you will not tell me without some persuasion. Fortunately we have everything we need, here at hand.' He waved his thick fingers towards torture implements around the walls of the place.

Turning his head, he snapped something in Russian to the men behind him and one of them moved forward to stand behind Carradine's chair. His fingers, strong and pliable, moved around the other's neck, found a nerve there and pressed sharply. An agony of pain lanced through Carradine's body, from his head to his toes. He jerked and thrashed in the chair, held there by the restraining leather straps. Savagely, he bit down on the cry of pain that rose to his lips. His eyes squeezed themselves tightly shut. Sweat boiled out on his forehead and along the small of his back.

How long it went on, he had no way of telling. To him, it seemed like an eternity, although in reality it was probably no longer than five minutes. The man behind him knew his job perfectly. It was clear he had almost surgical knowledge of the precious spots in the human body, knew just where to find them and the right amount of pressure to bring to bear on them to provide the maximum amount of pain. Carradine closed his eyes tightly until red and yellow flashes began to shoot in front of them. Deliberately, he tried to slow down his great breathing. He had read that the fakirs of India could shut out all pain by simply controlling their breathing and pulse rate. But holding his breath only seemed to make it worse. The torment stabbed and lanced through his limbs as he writhed in the chair.

At length, when it seemed he could hold out no longer, the fat man issued a harsh command. The torment ceased. The man moved away from him, resumed his place behind Kreznikov's chair. There was absolutely no expression on his face. He had simply been carrying out an order given to him by a superior authority and the fact that he had been torturing a man had no place in his thoughts. The ideal man to have around when you want to question anyone, Carradine thought weakly.

'Really, this is most regrettable,' went on the smooth, bland voice. 'It is also utterly unnecessary. You are going to tell me everything I want to know. Your name. Why you are here. Who sent you. If I do not get the answers to these questions one way, be sure I shall get them in another. This is only making things more difficult and painful for you. Don't you see that?'

Carradine shook his head from side to side, his body hanging forward against the straps. It felt as though he had been pummelled by some ham-fisted Swedish masseur and then trampled on by a rampaging elephant. Slowly, he forced himself erect, sobbing air down into his chest. There did not seem to be a single square inch of his body that had escaped the scientific punishment meted out by the hatchet-man.

A door in the wall behind Kreznikov, at the top of a short flight of stone steps, opened. The man who came in and walked down towards them was of the same anonymous shape. Why did these Russians always look so similar? Was it a national trait, or did Englishmen all look alike to them?

The man paused behind Kreznikov's chair, bent and whispered something in his ear. Dully, Carradine watched. Something had undoubtedly happened, otherwise Kreznikov would not have been interrupted in this fashion.

Carradine saw the other's head lift; the dark, empty eyes stared at him, and there was a faint expression of recognition in them. Kreznikov said in a voice edged with a fresh interest: 'So, you are Stephen Carradine. Forgive me for not recognising you earlier.' He nodded his head slowly. 'Now I understand a great many things. The British Secret Service would naturally be very interested in Professor Ubyenkov and his process.' He paused, then went on: 'This alters my plan quite a lot. The man, Nerim, means nothing to me. He will have to be removed. I have little doubt that the Communist Party in Bulgaria will be glad of his permanent removal. He has proved to be a thorn in their side for too long. But for you, I have something very special. We have a man in

Moscow who would like very much to question you.' His lips twitched back in a smile of anticipation. No doubt, thought Carradine, he was looking forward to receiving some special award for bringing him back to Moscow.

'Then you do not intend to kill me now?' Carradine asked quietly. It was suddenly, desperately urgent that he should know. He could do nothing but die, but he preferred to die fighting and on his feet if it were necessary. However, if he was not to die just yet, almost any later opportunity for resistance would be less suicidal than this.

'Not yet,' murmured the other. He got to his feet. 'You will be my honoured guest back in Moscow. Perhaps it would be better for you if I were to get one of my men to shoot you now.' He smiled ominously. 'They have ways of dealing with enemy spies in Moscow.'

* * *

There was a faint, panting hum in Carradine's ears as he sat tensed in the

164

chair. He had heard it for some time now, but it had only just dawned on him what it was. They would have to have an electrical generator somewhere in this place to provide them with the light and power they needed. Judging from the sound and the faint throbbing that he could feel through the soles of his feet, it was very close.

He leaned back and tried to find a comfortable position so that he was able to relax. He knew that the Russian counter-espionage agency was good, but this had certainly been excellent as far as he was concerned. They had managed to play on the superstitious ways of these people and take over this entire region. How long it had been in existence like this he did not know. It may have been one of their lookout places, deliberately set up to keep an eye on the Bulgarian people, especially after the abortive Hungarian Revolution. It did not seem likely that it had all been set up immediately after Ubyenkov was known to be in the area. Not even the Russians would have been able to work so fast, putting in all of the necessary equipment. Possibly, too, it was intended as a listening outpost on Turkey, one of the members of the Western Alliance, and a very close neighbour of Russia's.

Looking across at the man who sat in the chair near the door, he wondered what chance there was of getting the other close enough for him to make a grab for the gun. They had untied his arms, but his legs were still strapped to the chair. He flexed his fingers and saw the other's head jerk up even at that slight movement, the gun in his hand swinging around so that the round black hole in the barrel lined up to his chest.

The man grinned. 'Ostorozhno!' he said tightly.

Carradine tensed, then forced himself back. No chance at all. The other would have given him his orders, to stay where he was and take no chances. Even though he held the gun and with his animal-like intelligence and cunning, he would do just that, nothing more and nothing less.

They had taken away his own gun, had even removed the small knife blade that had been concealed in the heel of his shoe. They had not, however, thought to relieve him of the cigarette lighter and case. They both rested in his pockets, but would he get the chance to use them? They were now his only chance.

How long he sat there it was impossible to tell. His watch had been smashed sometime before, the one he had got from Nerim to replace that which had been broken when the car had gone over the edge of the road. Two wristwatches in as many days, he thought with grim amusement. What would the Chief say if he ever got back to put in a claim for them both?

The panting murmur of the generator grew louder for an instant. The door at the head of the stone steps had opened, a gaping black mouth through which Kreznikov stepped a few seconds later. He came slowly down the steps and gave an order to the guard.

The man got swiftly to his feet, pulled a knife from his pocket and stepped forward. For a second, Carradine had the feeling that this was surely the end, that

Kreznikov had been playing with him all of this time, that he had never intended to take him back to Moscow as a prisoner, but had meant to finish him permanently. Then the guard bent, slashed at the thongs that held his ankles and stepped back. The knife disappeared as swiftly as it had come and the gun was back in the other's hand, levelled on him as he leaned forward, ignoring the man while he rubbed his ankles where the skin had been torn and bloodied. Slowly, the feeling was restored.

'We are ready to leave now,' Kreznikov said softly. 'Professor Ubyenkov, the man you came to rescue, is outside. Needless to say, he will not be going to the West as he fondly imagined. The men who helped him here were stupid, bungling amateurs. They have been disposed of.'

Carradine stretched himself, aware that the two men were watching his every move closely. This might be the only chance he would get and he had to play his hand very cautiously indeed. The slightest suspicion on their part and it would all come to naught.

'I suppose you have no objection if I smoke one last cigarette,' he said calmly.

Kreznikov eyed him narrowly, then shrugged and slid his gaze to where the guard was watching very closely. He nodded finally. 'I suppose not,' he said, smiling faintly. 'It is one of your curious English traits that you must have a cigarette before going to your doom. The stiff upper lip. The public school image. You seem to consider that this image gives you a far higher standing in the eyes of the rest of the world. Nothing, my friend, could be further from the truth. It makes you appear as soft and degenerate as you really are.'

'I'm glad you have such a high opinion of us.' Moving his hand very slowly and carefully, he took the slender gold cigarette case from his pocket and held it in his hand for a moment. Opening it, he took out one of the Turkish cigarettes that Volescu had given him and placed it between his lips. There was a taut stillness in the room, so quiet that even above the panting hum of the distant generator, he could hear the thudding of his own heart against his ribs. Pray God that Kreznikov couldn't.

'Be very careful,' said the other quietly. His eyes never once left Carradine's face. 'If you make one move that I don't like, Mischa here will shoot you. Not to kill. Perhaps in the shoulder and then in the knee. Both can be extremely painful and crippling, I assure you. Such a high price to pay for a moment of folly.'

'I agree.' Carradine nodded. He saw the guard take two paces towards him. The muzzle of the snub-nosed automatic did not waver by so much as a millimetre in the stone-like fist. He put his left hand casually into his pocket and pulled out the lighter. If it worked as Forbes had claimed it would, then he had a chance. A slim, fantastically remote chance, but a slender hope for all that.

Flicking the lighter, he applied the flame to the end of the cigarette, inhaled deeply with a sigh of such obvious enjoyment that Kreznikov actually smiled broadly, and made to say something.

Blowing the smoke out of his mouth, Carradine turned the lighter over in his

170

hand, his thumb resting on the short arm of metal. Swiftly, he clicked it again. The thin, colourless spray of liquid struck the guard full in the face. He reeled back, throwing up an arm as he was temporarily blinded. Even though he had known what to expect, Carradine felt a faint sense of surprise at the speed with which the chemical worked. Choking and gasping, the other went down onto his knees, the gun falling from suddenly nerveless fingers as he tried to claw at his eyes. Ignoring him now, knowing there was nothing to fear from him at the moment, Carradine moved towards Kreznikov. The man was standing absolutely motionless, taken completely by surprise at what had happened. He opened his mouth to shout a warning, but the yell died in a gurgling moan as the spray hit him in the face. His eyes were screwed up in the broad, fleshy face; his mouth was open, revealing broken teeth; the tongue thrust forward as the vapour of the chemical, inhaled into his lungs, paralysed the respiratory muscles.

Ignoring the pain of returning circulation in his legs, Carradine jumped over the two convulsed, twitching bodies and ran up the stone steps. At the door he paused and pressed himself up momentarily into it, still clutching the cigarette case in his hand. Deftly, he turned the initialled monogram on the front. There was a soft click and the long blade of the knife flicked out like the tongue of a striking snake. He had planned for a man to be watching Ubyenkov but, as he stepped through into the long stone chamber with the huge generator set in one corner, humming out its endless rhythm of power, he saw that there were two men with the slight figure of the professor. It was too late to go back for one of the guns in the other room.

He lunged forward and came upon the two guards before they were aware of his presence. They had been expecting nothing. Both were taken by surprise. The first man swung round but was seconds too late. Carradine's fist, holding tightly onto the case, thrust forward beneath the man's upraised arm. The blade was slid between his ribs without any resistance and the man collapsed with a high-pitched wailing cry that was terrible to hear.

The man gave a convulsive twist as he pitched to the uneven floor and the move jerked the knife from Carradine's hand. Before he could recover himself, the other guard was on him. Not pausing to use any gun he may have had on his person, the other threw himself forward, hands reaching out to Carradine's throat. The fingers curled around his neck, the thumbs against the windpipe, pressing down with all of the man's strength behind them. Through the haze that wavered in front of his vision, Carradine saw the terrible face, the lips drawn back in a bestial smile, all teeth, eyes wide and glaring. Forced back by the other's superior weight, Carradine lashed out with the toe of his shoe and felt it strike the other's shin just above the left knee, but for all the effect that it had on the man he might just as well have saved himself the effort. The fingers tightened on his throat and it was impossible for him to draw air down into his oxygen-starved lungs. The bright light that hung suspended from the roof blurred, and seemed to sway in a wide circle as his stupefied vision began to fade.

His scrabbling fingers clawed for the man's wrists and strove to pull them apart, but the other held on grimly, forcing him back until he was jammed tightly against the rugged stone wall, an out-thrusting knob of rock pressing painfully into the small of his back just above the kidney.

Nails tore at his flesh as the man increased the pressure. There was a roaring in his head that drowned out the noise of the generator and the harsh rasp of their breathing. Then, suddenly, the grip of the hands around his throat loosened. There was a dull thud, a sickening crunch and the body that was holding him down fell away. Strangling on his own breath as he strove to draw it into his lungs, Carradine blinked his eyes. Tears blinded him for an instant and it was impossible for him to see anything through the red blur that danced in front of his eyes. Slowly, his vision cleared. The guard lay slumped at his feet, arms and legs outspread. There was a dull smear of blood on the back of his head. A short distance away, the professor stood staring with a look of stupefied amazement at the heavy piece of rock he held in his right hand.

'I had to hit him,' he said in a low, hushed voice. His English was far from perfect, but understandable. 'Otherwise he would have killed you.'

'There was nothing else you could do.' Carradine nodded, caught the other by the arm and hurried him away from the spot. 'But now we must get out of here before someone decides to come along and see what is happening.'

Two brightly lit underground rooms, one filled with the most bizarre equipment that Carradine had ever seen. What a pity there was no way of destroying all of this. But time was precious and his instructions had been to get Ubyenkov out of the country. Everything else had to be secondary. He did not doubt that Kreznikov and his henchmen would come after them in a very short time. Beyond the second lighted room, they found themselves facing a wide, dark tunnel that led downward into the rock beneath the ruins. Was it the same one along which he had climbed with Nerim?

Coolly, unhurriedly, he urged the other forward. There was sweat on the man's face and he was breathing heavily. It was not going to be easy for Ubyenkov to keep up this pace for long, but there was no other choice open to them. It was run or be caught. He guessed that the other would be fully aware of the consequences of being caught.

There was a thin twittering in the darkness on either side of them as they ran along the dark tunnel. Not a glimmer of light showed and they kept a tight grip on each other as they ran, stumbling and falling over the uneven ground. By the time they reached the end of the tunnel, their legs and arms were bleeding in several places where they had crashed on to the sharp rock. In front of them, there was a pale purple glow, a little lighter than the rocky walls which still hemmed them in.

Now minutes were precious. No time to waste making up his mind which track they ought to take. It had been clear from the very beginning that a man in Ubyenkov's condition would never be able to tackle that twisting winding ledge, that hideous descent around the great bulging overhang. They would have to take the usual track down the slope and trust that they reached the bottom before any of Kreznikov's men came after them.

There was no sign of the moon when they came out into the open air. Behind them, the walls of the castle loomed dark and forbidding against the clear, star-strewn heavens. And swiftly, without pausing or breaking their stride, they ran for the wide track that led down from the castle. Ubyenkov's breath was rasping harshly in his throat, but he kept manfully on, matching strides with Carradine.

They reached a turn in the track. Carradine threw a swift glance over his shoulder. Was that a light that had suddenly appeared in one of the glassless windows of the castle? He tried to make it out more clearly, but could not be sure. If it was, then it was more than likely that their escape had been discovered, that Kreznikov or that killer of his had recovered from the paralysing effect of the tear gas that he had used on them, that already the orders were being given. Even here in Balchik, he and Ubyenkov would not be safe. Not only would the Red killers be after them, but Kreznikov would not hesitate to inform the police authorities of what had happened and they would have them on their trail too. Somehow, they had to get out of Balchik. It might just be possible that Nerim's men would help him by creating a diversion to cover their escape, even if they had to know that Nerim himself was dead. Inwardly, Carradine no longer doubted this. Somehow, the other had been forced to tell Kreznikov and his men of Carradine's identity and once he had done that, he would be of no further use to the enemy. They would kill him with as little thought as they would of swatting a fly.

Now they were running along the track very close to the cliff edge. Down below them, the dull waters of the Black Sea lay like a dark mirror, reflecting very little from their depths. Ubyenkov stumbled and would have fallen had not Carradine instinctively tightened his grip on him. Even as he helped the other to his feet, there came an unmistakable sound from up the hill behind them. A car engine starting up. They would be on them in less than two minutes. Far below, it was just possible to make out the clustered lights of Balchik. Too far for them to hope to reach it in time.

He stared about him swiftly. There was, perhaps, only one chance. Close at hand lay a heap of large, tumbled boulders, scattered at random on the far side of the track. Urgently, he shouted to Ubyenkov: 'Help me to get those rocks into place. Quickly!'

Desperately, his hands fumbled with one of the large rocks, heaving it over the rough ground, planting it in the middle of the road. He motioned to the other to pull more across, setting them in a slight curve over one half the road, the half further away from the edge of the cliff. The rocks, he knew, were large enough for the driver of the car to spot them as he came around the corner. It was essential the man behind the wheel should see the obstruction just in time. Carradine did not want the car to go straight over the rocks, as he knew the distance from the bend to that point was far too short to give the man any chance to pull up. Instinct would take over. He would do what ninety-nine men out of a hundred would do in those circumstances. He would forget completely about the sheer drop to the left. Instead, he would automatically swerve in that direction at the same time taking his foot off the accelerator and ease down on the brake.

'That's it,' Carradine said hoarsely. The sound of the car engine was much closer now and a split second later, the great beams of the headlights flashed out, dancing over the rocks as the car bounced its way swiftly down from the castle. 'Into the rocks.'

They crouched down among the rugged boulders that lined the right-hand edge of the track. The car came on inexorably. The light from the searchlight swung around the bend first, then the car, low and black. Carradine caught a brief glimpse of the men in it; there were at least six, possibly seven. Unsuspecting men, not knowing that death lay so close to them, hovering like a black but invisible shape in the night.

The driver caught a fragmentary glimpse of the rocks stretched out across most of the track. Through narrowed eyes, Carradine saw him swing hard on the wheel, reacting just as he had reckoned he would. Now the brakes. There was the screech of rubber bleating protestingly on the rock, then the front of the car slewed sideways, and kept on swinging. One of the men in the front of the car had time to fling an arm up in front of his face in a futile attempt to ward off the danger that now loomed terrifyingly upon them. Then the car hurtled out into the darkness beyond the edge of the cliff. There was the savage rending sound of metal striking the out-jutting ledges of rock all the way down the sheer side of the cliff. Moving out across the track, stepping carefully as he came to the spot where the wheels of the car had gouged twin tracks through the soft, crumbly earth on the lip of the track, he peered down, aware that Ubyenkov had moved forward and was standing by his shoulder.

They were just in time to see the car tumble over the rocks at the very bottom the cliff, heading down for the water. Something black and oddly shapeless, like a rag doll, was flung clear and hurled into the water. Then the black shape of the car struck. The sound of the splash reached them seconds later and the white-foamed waves rippled together, covering the submerged car. Five minutes later, the surface of the sea was as calm and as undisturbed as it had been before.

* * *

'You say that Nerim is dead?' The thin-faced man stared at Carradine across the top of the desk, his features white in the pale flickering glow of the single lamp on the desk. 'How did he die?' There was little feeling in the voice, no accusation, yet Carradine had the inescapable feeling that somehow the other blamed him for Nerim's death.

'I don't know. There's a whole nest of Russian agents up there in the castle, led by a man called Aleksandre Kreznikov. We were jumped before we had a chance. Even then I thought they might have been the men who were keeping Ubyenkov here. It didn't take me long to realise my stupid mistake. They were questioning Nerim and myself individually. I refused to tell them anything, but evidently Nerim told them who I was. I think they must have killed him once they found out that. Kreznikov informed me that they had quite a file on him, that they knew everything there was to know of him.'

'So he is dead then. What do you want us to do?'

Patiently, Carradine said: 'They sent a car full of men after us when we were on our way down the cliff. We stopped them, rather permanently, I'm afraid. But there will be others. They cannot afford to let us get out of Bulgaria alive. Is there any transport I can have to get us back to Kazanluk?'

'Yes, there is a car. But whether you will be able to outrun them, I don't know.'

'If you could fill it with petrol and let me have it as soon as possible, I'll have a dammed good try.'

'Very well. I do not doubt that this is what Nerim would have wished had he been here. I will see to it at once.'

Carradine sat back in the chair, arms hanging loosely by his side. Across the desk, Ubyenkov stared at him out of dull, opaque eyes.

'Do you really think you have a chance against these men? You do not realise the full extent of their organisation. It is like the tentacles of a giant octopus. It stretches across all parts of Europe, possibly further. Although you might get me to Paris, you cannot be sure that you are safe even there.'

'We'll be a damn sight safer than we are here,' Carradine declared harshly. 'Besides, I know a man in Kazanluk who will give us all the help we need. He has been fighting these men for many years, certainly since the war ended.'

'Very well. I will go with you. Even

though I do not think you will succeed. But there is no other choice open to me. I committed myself the moment I fled from Russia. The moment I gave word of my intentions to one of your men.'

'In London, they are glad that you did. We need the details of this process of yours urgently. It's absolutely vital that I get you to London.'

The other smiled faintly. 'It is nice to know that one's work is appreciated outside his own country,' he said.

'You'll have all of the facilities you need once we get to England,' Carradine promised. 'Besides, there will be — ' He broke off suddenly. There came an abrupt diversion. The door at the far end of the room burst open and someone came in. Carradine swung sharply in his chair and got to his feet in surprise.

'Steve! I thought it was you. Have you got — ?' Francesca Romano glanced at the man in the other chair, then nodded her head quickly. 'I see that you have. Quickly, we must get out of Balchik at once.'

'I know.' She was the last person

Carradine had expected to see, yet it made sense. She had warned him in a friendly way that she had more information than he had, when they had parted in Kazanluk and when she had driven off, she had headed in this direction. But he had beaten her to Ubyenkov. He felt a brief sense of exultation. The rivalry had been of a friendly nature, yet it had been a serious thing. 'A car is being got ready to take us to Kazanluk. Once we get there we can — '

'Don't be a fool, Steve.' There was a trace of biting scorn in her voice now. Then her face softened. 'I'm sorry. I should have realised that you must have gone through a lot to get him out of there. But the first place they will head for is Kazanluk. You don't realise how big they are, how they work. They know everything of Volescu and the men working for him. They know that he is a man you'll turn to for help. You'll be killed long before you get there. I have my car outside. Come with me and we'll be across the frontier before dawn. They'll never catch up with us.'

It made sense. Carradine was forced to admit that. He cursed himself inwardly for not having considered that before. He would have driven off blindly to Kazanluk and when there was no sign of pursuit, blandly believed himself to be safe while all the time, a message would have been flashed from Balchik to Kazanluk, describing Ubyenkov and himself in minute detail and there would be a welcoming committee waiting for him, possibly just this side of Kazanluk so that Volescu would not have the chance to interfere and make things awkward for the Reds.

The thin-faced man who had been standing on one side listening to all this nodded. 'It is better that you should do as she says,' he said quickly. 'It is your only chance. If those men come here I shall tell them you left for Kazanluk. That is what they are expecting and I think they will believe me.'

Carradine did not want to hear any more. Seconds, not minutes, were precious now. He followed Francesca out of the warehouse, with Ubyenkov close on his heels. The car was there, waiting.

There was no sign of the man who had been with her when they had met on the road outside of Zlatica. She slid in behind the wheel and pressed the starter as they both got in, Ubyenkov in the back.

Moments later, they slithered away from the dark pavement, out through the maze of narrow streets, then along the main street and headed along a road which was to take them north-west. As they topped a low rise, Carradine caught his last glimpse of the grim, forbidding ruins of the castle, perched on top of the cliff, over to the right. It loomed dark and grotesque in the dimness, just visible in the faint starshine. There was no sign of life there, but in his mind's eye, he could visualise the activity that was going on there that moment, with Kreznikov issuing his orders, sending out commands. No doubt the other knew the consequences of his failure to hold Ubyenkov once he had him in his hands. No allowance was made for mistakes in Moscow.

6

BETWEEN TURTUCAIA
AND OLTENITA

There was no pursuit. Carradine had been more than half-expecting it and when it failed to materialise by the time they drove through Tolbukhin shortly before three o'clock in the morning, he knew that either the girl had been right in her assumption that Kreznikov would not expect them to head in this direction, or the other had taken no chances and had passed his message along to the frontier which, if his memory served him well, was somewhere between Turtucaia and Oltenita.

As they drove, he gave the girl a graphic account of what had happened since they had parted in Kazanluk. She listened attentively while keeping her concentration on the road ahead. In the inky blackness, it was difficult to drive and in places the road wound and twisted to such an extent that he would have felt better with snow chains on the wheels.

'Do you know this man Kreznikov?' he asked when he had finished recounting his story to her.

'I have heard of him,' she said quietly. 'He's from Kazakhstan. A fiend. I'm not surprised that they put him in charge of this operation to get the professor back to Russia. It's a great pity that you did not kill him when you had the chance. The world would have been a far better place.'

'I'm afraid there wasn't time in which to think of that. I had to get the professor away from there and there was very little opportunity for doing it. If I'd stopped to take care of Kreznikov and his men I might never have made it. As it was, I managed it only by the skin of my teeth.'

'How many men are left now?'

'Up there at the castle, you mean?' Carradine shook his head. 'I'm afraid I have absolutely no idea. Two men were killed in the castle when we got away, and another six or seven were accounted for when their car went over the edge. But for

190

all I know, he may have had an army of men up there. Certainly no one in Balchik would have been any the wiser. Nerim did not mention them to me so he could not have known.'

'I see. Somehow, I doubt if there are many more unaccounted for. He will be forced to telephone most of his orders now. They have cells all over the country. He may send word though to Turtucaia, although I doubt it. It would be insane for us to try to escape into Romania. Our plight would be just as bad there as it is here. He will argue that our best chance is back to Kazanluk and then through to Sofia, or better still, to try to head for the Turkish border. There we could be reasonably safe.'

'I hope you're right.' Carradine settled down into the seat of the car, allowing himself the pleasure of relaxing his taut muscles. 'I've been through too much tonight to have to face up to them again.'

The girl gave a brief nod. She glanced down at the speedometer, estimating the number of kilometres they had travelled since leaving Balchik. 'We still have quite a way to go before we get close to the frontier,' she said, with a trace of concern in her voice. 'I'll wake you before we reach there. You can trust me.'

Carradine leaned his head against the inside of the door, closed his eyes, then opened them again. 'There's one thing I forgot to tell you,' he said harshly. 'That man who was in Tamariu, the fat man who took you away in the boat — '

'Yes, what of him?' For a second, he thought he detected a note of fear in her voice.

'He was back there in Balchik. Nerim and I saw him. He was following us when we made our way through the outskirts on our way to the castle. He tried to shoot Nerim, but missed. He managed to get away along one of the alleys before I could get in a shot at him.'

The girl let out her breath in a quiet hiss through her tightly clenched teeth. But when she spoke, her voice was even, without a tremor. 'So he is still alive. I thought he was dead. If he succeeds in following us, I shall have to make certain the next time.'

The utter coldness in her tone sent a little shiver through Carradine. He did not like to hear women speak like that. He had always looked upon women as feminine creatures whose heads were filled with thoughts of love, of fashion, fast cars and adventure, but not of cold-blooded murder such as Francesca was suggesting now. Still, he thought wearily to himself, as he closed his eyes once more, she was in the same dangerous, and often dirty, businesses he was; and he knew only too well that it was a rat race of the most deadly kind, and one was often forced to kill to stay alive. The other side was playing for keeps and it was no child's game, even though on the surface it often seemed like one. Cops and robbers, but with real bullets and sudden death that struck without warning from the shadows.

Settling himself down against the springs of the seat, the purr of the wheels on the road a faintly heard background noise, he closed his eyes again, shutting out the hypnotic sway of the headlights as they lifted and fell rhythmically to the bumps and depressions in the road. He fell asleep almost at once.

★ ★ ★

The faint shudder as the car slid to a halt woke Carradine an interminable time later. He stirred himself, came wide awake at once and pushed himself upright, peering through the windscreen of the car. It was a grey dawn now, with most of the western sky still dark and a few of the brighter stars just visible.

'Where are we?' he asked hoarsely.

'We passed through Turtucaia five minutes ago. Oltenita is just across the Danube.'

'Are there any bridges across where they won't have frontier guards?'

The girl considered that for a moment and then shook her head. 'It's unlikely. But leave this to me.'

Carradine said seriously: 'You think you can talk your way through the Romanian frontier guards?'

'If they haven't been alerted by Kreznikov, I think I can.' There was a fresh note of confidence in her tone. 'I know these men. There have been times when we have had dealings with them. They are inclined to turn a blind eye to things like this provided they get some kind of recompense.'

Carradine did not bother to ask how much she intended to give them as a bribe to let them through. The Deuxieme Bureau probably provided its agents with an almost unlimited amount of funds whenever they were engaged on a mission of such vital importance as this. The big trouble was that Kreznikov might have more funds at his back then they had, and they were far closer to Russia than they were to France. If Kreznikov had managed to get word through the telephone to the frontier posts in this area, then they were finished and no amount of sweet talk from Francesca would get them through.

They drove around a wide, sweeping S-bend. In front of them, the still waters of the Danube stretched from left to right. The frontier post here loomed up out of the dim greenness and the girl brought the car to a halt at the posts. A plainclothes man stepped forward from the small building on the side of the bridge. There were two uniformed men close by, rifles held in their hands. They looked like sullen, suspicious men. A car driving here at this time of the morning was bound to arouse suspicion, he thought as he sat back. One hand rested on the slim cigarette case in his pocket. An ineffective weapon under these circumstances, but the best he had. He wondered whether the girl had a gun anywhere.

Leaning out of the window of the car, Francesca handed her papers to the plainclothes man and said something in Bulgarian, her voice deliberately pitched low as though intending that only he should hear her and not the two uniformed men standing nearby, their eyes watching everything. The plainclothes man nodded, examined the papers, then thrust them back. He retained a hold on a small wad that looked like bank notes. Then, turning, he snapped a sharp order; one of the uniformed men moved back into the building and a second later, the barrier was lifted and they were motioned through.

Slowly, Carradine let the breath whistle through his teeth. That was the first obstacle successfully passed. They still had to go through the checkpoint on the Romanian side of the river. If the girl had showed any anxiety about this, she certainly did not show it outwardly.

In second gear, they drove over the bridge towards the checkpoint. Again, there was the same procedure. Another short speech, this time presumably in Romanian, and then they were allowed to proceed. It seemed utterly incredible, yet they were through and inside Romania.

'I won't ask you how you managed that,' Carradine said softly. 'Because to me it was little short of a miracle. I only wish you would pass on that incantation to me for future use.'

'I'm afraid it might not be of any help to you,' she said, smiling a little. 'Unless you had the money to go with it.'

'And a pretty face,' Carradine remarked. 'I suppose that helps.'

'With some of them, it does,' she said

softly. 'Money and influence. Even here you will find the police officials can be bribed. They are often so poorly paid that these things are more common than you would imagine. Naturally they are very careful about those for whom they do it. But my name is known reasonably well here and some big talk to them sometimes opens many doors which would otherwise remain closed.'

'Of course.' Carradine nodded. 'Now that we are across the frontier and in Romania, what next? Or haven't you been thinking that far ahead?'

She gave him a sharp, oblique glance. 'Now you are making fun of me,' she said coldly. 'Of course I have been thinking. I know that we are still not safe. Once Kreznikov gets word from Kazanluk that we are not there, he will start thinking, and sooner or later it will occur to him that we may have slipped through his net into Romania. We must head for the Hungarian border where I also have friends. There it will be easy to move down into Yugoslavia or west into Austria.'

'It sounds all right,' murmured Carradine.

'Once in Austria, we can take the plane out to Paris,' the girl went on quickly, forcing home her point.

'Very well.' Seriously, Carradine said: 'But once we reach Paris, the professor comes with me to London by the first plane. I won't feel easy in my mind until I get him to London.'

The girl shrugged her shoulders delicately. Clearly she had been hoping that the Deuxieme Bureau might get a chance to question the other on their arrival in Paris, but she said nothing more and merely depressed her foot on the accelerator and let the car go.

'One other thing,' Carradine said. 'Do you have a gun anywhere? I feel naked without one.'

The girl hesitated, then inclined her head towards the glove compartment. 'There's one in there,' she said shortly.

Opening the compartment, Carradine found the small automatic. He took it out, checked that it was loaded, then slipped it in his pocket. He felt a little better now. The girl's charm and money had worked at the two frontier posts they had already passed through, but there was no cast-iron guarantee that they would pull strings for them next time.

Turning his head, he glanced into the rear seat. The professor was asleep, his head resting on the back of the seat, his mouth hanging open slightly. He must've been through more than they had. Let him sleep while he had the chance, he thought. There might be more trouble ahead for them and this might be the only opportunity he had.

Bucharest came and they stopped only long enough to fill the tank of the car with petrol and for a quick breakfast, a meal of silences, soon over. Even though he was outwardly calm, Carradine could smell the danger which surrounded them, still hanging close to them every second of this long journey. It was a physical thing, something he had known for a long time now and he had learned never to ignore. He was alive now and not dead in some dingy back alley, because he had known fear and it had somehow sharpened all of his senses. He was alive and some other men were dead because they had not been afraid, they had been so sure.

Leaving Bucharest, they drove north-west again, across Walachia, through the tiny, picturesque villages which dotted the roads, onto where the great, towering, snow-covered peaks of the Transylvanian Alps rose stark and tall against the vivid blue of the sky. Carradine recognised a few of them, as he took his spell at the wheel while the girl slept easily beside him, her head resting on his shoulder, that faint lingering perfume he had smelled so long ago at Tamariu in his nostrils.

Mount Mandra towered more than eight thousand feet above them with Retezat and Mount Gugu almost as high. He had once come here to ski more than eight years before, and he recalled gliding down those smooth slopes with the wind shrieking insanely in his ears and the smooth sound of the skis on the soft snow, his body crouched slightly as he leaned forward, exulting in the feeling of sheer speed.

But that was a long time ago, he thought with a faint sense of nostalgia. There was a part of his life that had been forgotten, swallowed in the welter of events that had followed so quickly on the heels of those long-lost and carefree days. Death and destruction had meant very little to him in those days. For some reason, the realisation sent a pang almost akin to pain through his body. How well the world spins backwards in the eye of memory, he thought a trifle sadly. But there was no sense in dwelling on the past. He had a task to perform and he would need all of his wits about him to carry it through to its successful conclusion.

There was a plan being built up against them somewhere and he wished he knew what it was. Kreznikov would have men watching for them throughout the whole length and breadth of the Balkans, and it was no use thinking otherwise. These men were no fools. He had worked against them long enough now to know how stupid it was to ever underestimate them or their organisation. The Soviet spy organisation was perhaps the most efficient in the world, and certainly the most ruthless. A man either made no mistakes, or he was removed, quickly and permanently. It was as simple as that.

It was late afternoon before they drew close to the frontier with Hungary at Salonta Mare. Francesca had chosen this point for crossing over and Carradine had not argued with her. After all, she had already shown that she knew what she was doing and he realised that if they were to get out of the Balkans safely, he would have to trust her completely. Only when they got to Paris would he have to keep his eyes open and his wits about him, or she would do her best to spirit Ubyenkov off to the Deuxieme Bureau and grab all the credit for herself. He could just imagine what the Chief would say if he allowed that to happen.

There was no difficulty getting past the guards on the Romanian side of the border. Evidently the girl had not been boasting in vain when she had said that money and influence talked as far as these men were concerned. Besides, reflected Carradine, it was unlikely that they would care about anything that was being taken out of Romania. There would be men on the other side who might have orders to watch for anyone bringing stuff into Hungary. But these Balkan states were all alike. In spite of what they claimed outwardly, there was just as much guile and corruption in high places here as anywhere else in the world.

The hard-faced Hungarian guards scrutinised their papers closely, took their time with the forged ones that Ubyenkov carried, then spoke rapidly with the girl. For several moments, there was a heated conversation, which Carradine did not understand. He knew only a word or two of Hungarian, but he guessed that Francesca was warning them as she had the others, that she had contacts in Hungary, men who could make things difficult for these men. Eventually, they were allowed to go on. Sitting back in his seat, Carradine relaxed his tight-fisted hold on the butt of the gun in his pocket and uncurled his stiff fingers.

They crossed the Black Crisul River. There was a flaring red sunset over Bekes, the beginning of a brilliant starlit night as they passed through Gyoma. Francesca was driving the car as if they were on a racetrack, but now there was some more traffic on the road and they were forced to slow on several occasions.

Sitting forward in his seat, Carradine said: 'I think we can take it easy now Francesca. We don't want to finish up in a ditch, not after we have got so far without any trouble.'

The girl gave him a sideways glance, then laughed softly. 'You sound as though you have very little confidence in my driving. It may interest you to know that my father was an international racing star back in the late thirties and some of his skill must have passed on to me.'

'All right. But don't take any unnecessary chances now. The way I see it, if Kreznikov had phoned through, he would have made a move before now. He can't afford to let others get too far. I'm beginning to think that he must have headed for Kazanluk, especially if those men in Balchik gave him the wrong information as they promised.'

'Men can be made to tell the truth,' said Ubyenkov from the back seat. 'They will not take their word as true. I know enough of Kreznikov to know that he will continue to hunt us down until we reach London. And, who knows, he may have men there too.'

'Relax. We'll get you through all right,' said the girl. There was something entirely new in her voice, a ring of confidence perhaps that had certainly not been there when Carradine had first met her at Tamariu. Leaning back in his seat, he turned his head slightly to watch her. She held that wheel in a completely relaxed way, even though the road was still treacherous in parts, with sharply angled bends coming on them quite unexpectedly out of the growing darkness. Her eyes were wide, sparking a little with the thrill of the excitement.

A white sign loomed up in the glare of the headlights. There was a sharp turn to the right and the girl took it fast. For a moment, the car went into a skid, then straightened out again as Francesca eased her foot off the accelerator pedal. They glided down the sloping, winding road that led down into a broad valley and out onto the Hungarian plains.

It was now completely dark, the last shred of colour having vanished from the sky. They passed through a small village, a cluster of houses that showed briefly on both sides of the road as the light of the headlights played over them. Coming out of the village, they passed a couple of slow-moving cars, the girl blaring the horn at them as she roared past.

Ten kilometres further on, motoring across the flat smoothness of the planes, Carradine glanced back through the rear window. Behind them, the road lay in utter blackness. Not a single light showed anywhere. It was almost as if they were moving at a snail's pace along the bottom of a deep well, shut in by the night and —

Suddenly he woke up from his reverie. The darkness was not quite absolute. There were lights behind them, just visible, winking on and off in an oddly inexplicable manner. Seconds passed before he realised what he was seeing: the twin headlights of another car, moving swiftly along the road that led down from the mountains, vanishing whenever the car took one of the hairpin bends, reappearing when they came out into the straight.

Not one of the cars they had passed just outside that tiny village. He felt sure of that. Neither of those two cars would have been capable of the speed at which this one was clearly travelling. Now there was an urgent question in his mind, one which might have to be answered very quickly.

He turned his head back to speak to the girl, but she forestalled him.

'I know,' she murmured quietly. 'I've just seen them in the mirror. What do you think? Some of Kreznikov's men?'

'It could be. If it is, they seem to be gaining on us steadily.'

'I know. And we're running short of petrol again. Maybe we should have filled a can with us the last time.'

'How far before we can get any more?'

The girl pursed her lips. 'Mezotur is the next place of any size. We should be there in fifteen minutes. Here's hoping that we find some place open this time of night.'

7

HUNGARIAN RHAPSODY

The twin lights, glaring now in the darkness, rising and falling in tune to the unevenness of the road, were much closer now. In spite of the fact that they were driving over the plain, it was tricky, undulating ground and in front of them were occasional ugly patches of midnight shadow which might have been breaks in the road, forcing the girl to drive carefully, to check on the brakes at all of them. Slowly, but inexorably, the car at their backs was overhauling them.

'We'll never make it to Mezotur,' he said after a few moments of tense silence. 'They're coming up much too fast now. Whoever it is driving that car he certainly knows the road.'

'We may be wrong about them,' Francesca said tautly. She spun the wheel sharply and they skidded around a bend that loomed up on them suddenly. The wind was a keening moan about the car now. There was a straight stretch in front of them which should allow them a good turn of speed, but it did not last long. The girl muttered something under her breath as the headlights, probing in front of them, picked out the climbing stretch of road that spiralled up the side of a low hill. No hope of driving fast up there. One wrong turn, one uncontrolled skid, and they were finished!

'You'd better think of something fast,' Francesca said, leaning forward a little, peering through the windscreen. 'They can't be more than a kilometre away now. They'll catch us within the next five minutes, long before we get to Mezotur.'

Turning in his seat, he threw a quick glance behind him, over Ubyenkov's shoulder. He noticed the other's white, strained face, then forgot it as he saw the flickering headlights of the other car glinting off the rocky banks of the road, suddenly spring into view around a corner just below them. He pulled himself a little more upright in his seat.

There was no longer any doubt at all in his mind as to who those men were.

The car lurched drunkenly as they swung around another hairpin bend. The girl was handling it beautifully and he felt a wave of thankfulness for the fantastic road-holding qualities of the car.

'Do you know this stretch of road at all?' he asked tightly.

'No. I've used it twice, but that's all.'

'We've only got one chance,' he said thinly. 'I thought I spotted the lights of a village just ahead, close to the top of the hill. There may be a side road leading off this one. Even if it's only a cart track it will do.'

'What's your plan?'

'As soon as we reach the village, slow down. This road twists and winds so much that the chances are we'll be out of sight of those men back there. If there is a side road leading off, drive into it and switch off all your lights, and the engine.'

'And if there isn't any side road?'

Very slowly, Carradine said: 'Then we'll have to try to fight them off. With just the one gun, we don't have much chance, I'm afraid. I'm sorry, but it's the only chance we have. These people have to stop us and they won't worry about waking up the village.'

There was a wide looping curve directly in front of them. As they swung round it, they saw the small cluster of lights less than a quarter of a kilometre away. Maybe a dozen or so houses, Carradine thought. The odds were fantastically against them. Even if they were lucky, even if there was a narrow alley into which they could drive and their pursuers missed them in the dark, it would only delay things for a little while. Sooner or later, those men would realise that they had been tricked. Then all they had to do was lie in wait for them somewhere along the road into Szolnok. But that was somewhere in the future. With effort, he concentrated all of his attention on the immediate problem.

The girl pressed down on the brake as they approached the village. It was bigger than Carradine had thought, the main road snaking up through it, on to the top of the hill, then down the other side.

Glancing back, he saw that the other car was out of sight, somewhere behind the bend.

'There!' Carradine shouted suddenly. He pointed to their left. The dark shadow of an opening between two of the low-roofed houses showed briefly as the headlights moved across it. The girl swung the car without a word. Tyres screeched on the road as they roared in the sharp turn. They scraped between the walls of the houses with scant inches to spare. Reaching forward, Francesca snapped off the lights and then switched off the ignition.

Carradine thrust open the door and felt it grate against the nearby wall. Somehow, he managed to squeeze through it. 'Wait here,' he snapped thinly. He edged his way along the side of the car, the rough wall scraping his arms and legs. Crouching down just inside the opening, the automatic in his right hand, he waited, holding his breath. Would this desperate plan succeed? In a few minutes that other car would come roaring through the village. Would they be driving fast enough to pass them before they realised there was an opening there? He tensed. In a few seconds, he would know.

The faint glimmer of powerful headlights reflected on the walls of the houses on the opposite side of the road showed in the darkness. In a second or so, the car would enter the village. The glow brightened. He heard the roar of the supercharged engine. That in itself told him more of the occupants of the car than anything else. There were very few cars with engines like that in Hungary. The secret police had a few and it was likely that Kreznikov and men such as he had also.

That ear-shattering roar rose to a sharp crescendo. The note changed as the car moved between the houses, the sound thrown back and magnified by the walls. He tightened his grip on the gun in his hand, the finger across the trigger, bar-straight and tensed. In a few more seconds, he thought tautly, a few more metres.

There was the sound of the gears being changed down. Was the driver suspicious?

Had he swung around the corner further down the road in time to see their tail-light vanish abruptly? Had he guessed what must have happened? The car drew level with him. The light reflected from the houses illuminated its interior with a pale glow, enabling him to see the man sat behind the wheel. For a moment, there was a faint sense of shock in Carradine's mind.

The first thing that struck him forcibly was that there was only one man in the car. He had been expecting Kreznikov to send at least half a dozen men after them. The second flash realisation, coming in a few seconds after the first, increased the tension in his mind and confirmed the fears which had been boiling up inside him. There was no mistake. The glow of the reflected light had been bright enough for him to recognise a round face, the hard, cruel mouth, the wide, square shoulders hunched forward over the wheel: the man he had first seen in the dining room of the hotel in Tamariu, a few seconds before he had been called to the phone, the man he had seen again in that little dingy alley in Balchik!

★ ★ ★

A lot had depended on how fast the other was going. Carradine had gambled on him driving like a bat out of hell in the attempt to catch them before they reached Szolnok, and it had come off. He got slowly to his feet as the roar of the powerful engine faded swiftly into the distance. The red tail-lights winked briefly, then vanished as the car drove over the top of the hill. How far the other would go before he realised that he was no longer following the scent, it was impossible to guess. Carradine did not believe that they could fool this man for long. He might decide to retrace his steps, or wait for them somewhere along the road. He might even lie in wait in Mezotur.

Francesca was still seated behind the wheel of the car. She had lit a cigarette and the pale orange glow was the only speck of light that illuminated the interior. It touched the lines of her face with shadow as she drew deeply on it, highlighting the cheekbones and the delicate structure of her features. As he slid into the seat beside her, she said softly, 'Well, what happened? Has it gone on?'

'I think so.' He nodded and took one of the cigarettes from the slender golden case. For a moment, his thumb brushed over the embossed monogram on the front and he felt a trace of grim tension in him. Would he ever have to use this thing again? he wondered. Flicking the lighter, he lit his cigarette and pulled the smoke down into his lungs gratefully.

'We will give him a few minutes and then drive on into Mezotur.' Sitting back, he turned things over in his mind. He said softly: 'I've been considering the situation, Francesca. I don't think it would be wise to try to take the plane out from Vienna. That's the way they will be expecting us to go.'

She turned to stare at him in surprise. 'But what other way is there? We can't possibly motor all the way across Europe.'

218

'No, I realise that.' There was a trace of impatience in his tone. 'We must take the train out to Paris.'

'The Orient Express. But they always watch that. If it isn't for smugglers, it's for people like us. I've been warned on several occasions never to take that train. It's far too risky.'

'Nevertheless, we must take that risk. I admit that it isn't as easy or as quick as taking the plane, but if our friends do try to follow us, we'll have a better chance of spotting them and doing something about it.' His words fell into a quiet hush. Even the professor had fallen silent in the back seat.

'I don't like it,' persisted the girl. 'By catching a plane for Vienna, we could be in Paris in two hours. It would take us almost two days on that train. The odds against us would be increased a hundred times.'

'Not at all,' said Carradine harshly. 'But we must have a chance to find out what these men are doing.' He tried to read the expression on her face. There was no clue there as to the nature of her thoughts. She smoked on the cigarette for a few more moments and then rolled down the window and tossed the stub out into the darkness.

She hesitated, then seemed to make up her mind. Reaching forward, she switched on the ignition and backed the car out onto the main road again, then spun the wheel and went through the village, her face set in a tight mask. Carradine sat back, wondering what he had said to upset her like that.

She did not seem to be the kind of girl who was so afraid of these people that she had to act in this way simply because he had suggested going on the train through Europe.

Maybe he had spoiled her plans for getting Ubyenkov back to France, for getting the Deuxieme Bureau to question him first. If that was the case that was just too bad, but he had his own orders and he intended to follow them to the letter. He reminded himself to be careful when they reached Paris.

Glancing sideways at the set of her jaw, he wondered if she was already scheming hard, looking for some way to turn the tables on him.

They found a garage open in Mezotur, filled up the tank and as an added precaution, took with them a jerry can filled to the brim with petrol. The town was still ablaze with light and although there was some traffic on the roads, there was no sign of the black car which had been following them most of the way until they had thrown it off.

* * *

With the girl sleeping by his side, Carradine sat behind the wheel and concentrated on staying awake. Through the windscreen he was able to make out the landscape on both sides of the winding road. It was now about two o'clock in the morning according to his reckoning. Without his watch he could make only rough estimates of the time but it had been twelve-fifteen when they had passed through Szolnok, and he guessed it was little over fifty kilometres from there to Budapest; the needle of the speedometer had stayed around the forty-five mark most of the way.

He jerked himself up in the seat, shifting his position in an effort to fight off the weariness in his body.

Beside him, the girl's head leaned against his arm, the warmth of her seeping through his coat. Once or twice, his head jerked forward, only for a split second, but long enough for his concentration to relax, to send the car over the very edge of the road. The movement would jerk him awake almost at once, with a cold sweat starting out on his forehead and along his spine, and his hands would move almost of their own volition to correct the swing. He screwed up his eyes tight and then opened them again, stifling a yawn. That scientific beating he had taken back there in the castle at Balchik had not made things any easier for him and he had had only a few hours' sleep since they had left the coast town and started out on this nightmare journey across Romania and Hungary. Now Budapest lay only a few kilometres ahead of them and God alone knew what further dangers lay in wait for them there. Was that man watching the airport, scanning the passenger lists, ready to move in if they put in an appearance, laying his plans accordingly? If he was, then by God he was going to be disappointed.

He guided the car around a sharp bend. They ran on between the tall trees of a dense stretch of forest. In places the branches closed in over their heads and made the night even darker than before. Out of the gloomy forest, over a ravine and then they were within sight of the ugly sprawl of Budapest, only a few lights showing at that unearthly hour of the morning.

★　★　★

It was still dark when the sharp-eyed Yugoslavian officials came aboard the train at the frontier. Most of them were plainclothes men and they examined their papers with a close scrutiny before handing them back, apparently satisfied. Carradine sat back in the seat and stared out from the window. By dawn, he estimated, they should be in Zagreb and although it was not an official stopping place for passengers on the Orient Express, the train did wait there for some time before proceeding on its journey into Northern Italy, and a little time was all they needed to get on board.

Once we get there and on board the Orient Express, the worst of it will be past, he thought to himself, staring at his own reflection in the glass. They had had fantastic luck on reaching Budapest. Leaving the car there, knowing that to continue using it was becoming more and more dangerous as time went on, they had made their way to the main station, to find that a train was already standing on the platform bound for Zagreb. This, Carradine had told the girl, was the kind of luck which came only through good living. He had said it with his tongue in his cheek and she had smiled faintly. He had the feeling that she was still angry with him for altering their plans in his abrupt manner but she had not demurred when they had climbed on board the

waiting train. Now both she and Ubyenkov were asleep again. They had the
compartment to themselves. Few people
seemed to be travelling on this train and
although Carradine had leaned from the
window and scanned everyone moving
along the platform at Budapest, there had
been no sign of the man who had been
tailing them. He felt a little easier in his
mind now. If the other was waiting at the
airport, expecting them to take the first
available flight for Paris, then he would
have a far longer wait than he anticipated.

The train hammered its way south now,
rolling through the Yugoslavian countryside. Through the window, Carradine
could see very little of it. An occasional
station flashed by, dark and shadowed,
accompanied by the red and green lights
of signals. But for the most part, they
thundered on through the pitch blackness
with only the faint gleam of the light from
the coach on the metal rails that ran
alongside them.

Shortly before dawn, the train rattled
and jostled its way across points, slowing
appreciably. Reaching forward, Carradine

shook the girl gently by the shoulder and saw her eyes flick open. For a second she stared about her with no recognition on her face, then she pushed herself upright and ran her fingers through her hair, brushing it back from her forehead.

'Where are we now?' she asked, glancing through the window where the dawn was just painting a grey streak across the eastern horizon.

'A few minutes out of Zagreb,' he told her. 'Better wake the professor. If the Orient Express isn't in the station, it soon will be.'

She nodded, turned and shook Ubyenkov's arm. He stirred, then came awake at once. Outside, they ran alongside a train of wagons in a long siding. Then the station came into view, squat and functional in the pale grey light. With a jolt, the train slid alongside the platform and came to a clanking halt. There was the shrill hiss of escaping steam forward of the train.

It was going to be another hot day, Carradine thought, standing on the dusty platform, looking up into the brightening sky. The air had a smoky smell as he drew in a great gulp of it, glancing along the platform. A few passengers had alighted and were moving towards the far end.

They waited on the platform until the last of the other passengers had disappeared. The official at the far gate watched them for a moment, then turned his back. There was a shrill whistle from the locomotive, the hiss of steam, and the wheels began to turn as it moved out of the station. As the last carriage passed in front of him, Carradine glanced across the rails and muttered a short curse through tight lips. There, less than fifty metres away, stood the Orient Express, between two lines of locomotives. Of course, since this was not a regular stop the train had been halted in one of the sidings. He caught the girl by the arm and motioned towards the train.

'There it is,' he said sharply. 'Stick close to me and let me do the talking this time.'

A quick glance told him that the man at the ticket gate was no longer interested in them. Running forward, they moved between the tall empty shells of the locomotives, many of them rusting away on the rails. Now these half-forgotten giants of the pre-war days hid them from the sight of anyone on the platform. By the time the official got to wondering where they were, they would be out of Zagreb and on their way to Ljubljana and the Italian border.

The through coaches of the Orient Express were clearly marked, most of them first-class sleeping compartments. These he avoided. They would have to travel hard the rest of the way. A pity, but it could not be helped.

In the all-prevailing greyness, they climbed on board. They would have to square things with the conductor, but Carradine did not foresee any difficulty there.

Less than five minutes later, the diesel gave a low moan and the train moved out between the rusted rails, the remnants of a bygone age, and Zagreb was left behind as the new day flamed over the Yugoslavian countryside. They waited until they were several kilometres away, then walked along the corridor until they found an empty compartment. Leaving the girl and the professor there, Carradine went to find the conductor. The other was in the small compartment at the very end of the coach. He listened sympathetically to Carradine as he explained that he and his two companions had to get to Paris as soon as possible owing to the serious illness of the girl's mother. There had been no time for them to buy tickets at Zagreb. Would it be possible for him to pay now?

Taking out his wallet, he deliberately opened it so that the wad of notes was clearly visible. The avaricious gleam in the conductor's eyes told Carradine that he had not made a mistake about the characters of the men who worked on these trains.

'Your passports are in order?' inquired the other officiously.

'Of course.' Carradine held them out for the other's inspection. It was obvious that the man did not have the first idea of what to look for in a forged passport. He gave the outward impression of studying them carefully, then handed them back.

'You realise, of course, that this is highly irregular. It should really be reported since Zagreb is not an official halt for the express, However — '

'I realise there may be difficulties, but I'm sure I can rely on you to smooth them out.' Carradine held out a wad of notes. 'This ought to pay for our tickets to Paris and also for your trouble.'

The conductor smiled broadly, took the money. 'I'll write you out your tickets right away.'

Going back to the compartment, he slid open the door, stepped inside and closed the door behind him. The girl looked up from her seat in the corner. There was an unspoken question in her eyes. Sitting down, Carradine said softly: 'Everything has been taken care of. I got our tickets from the conductor. All the way through to Paris.'

'So now all we have to do is wait,' said Ubyenkov with a faint sigh. 'I think that this is going to the hardest part for all of us. We are so near, and yet so far. This is how you English describe it, is it not?'

Carradine said seriously: 'As soon as it

gets light, I want to take a walk along this section of the train, just to be sure that we are all right. Knowing our Russian friends, there can always be trouble.'

'But how could they possibly know that we are on this train?' asked Ubyenkov.

'Whilst they don't have second sight any more than we do, they do have an extremely efficient organisation throughout this part of Europe. Even though we gave that man the slip last night, he could have passed word along once he discovered what we'd done. I'd say that the private lines were humming furiously all last night and this morning as they tried their hardest to trace us. I'd say they now have a pretty good idea of where we are. They've either got a man on this train, or there will be one joining it further along the line, possibly at Trieste.' Leaning back, he stared out from the window where the tall sky-rearing mountains of Slovenia lifted high against a brilliant blue sky. The air was fresh and clean here, free from the smoke of big towns, and by the time they had breakfasted in the small restaurant car, they had left Ljubljana behind and were heading towards Italy.

Carradine waited until they were through Sezana and the Yugoslavian officials had left before making his check on the rest of the train. They were now inside Italy and had just passed through Poggioreale. The train swayed continually from side to side as it rushed over the gleaming rails.

Glancing into the compartments, he eyed the occupants closely, searching for anything, any clue that would indicate danger. He knew most of the signs. The tourists were easily picked out, and dismissed from his mind just as quickly. The others, those who were either Yugoslavians or Italians, were a little more difficult to study and make up his mind about.

He reached the end of the third carriage when he paused, undecided, as he came to a compartment with the blind down. Now, how to see in there? It could mean nothing at all; but on the other hand, it was just possible that whoever was in there had a good reason for not wanting to be seen. He was on the point of moving on when the sound of footsteps moving along the corridor halted him and a second later, the conductor came into sight. He gave a brief smile as he recognised Carradine.

'I'm looking for a friend of mine who said he would be travelling on this train,' Carradine explained easily. 'I've seen nothing of him so far and I was wondering if he was in this compartment. I don't like to go in just in case it isn't him and — '

'Leave it to me.' The conductor took the money which Carradine slipped to him, and knocked sharply on the door while Carradine stood back along the corridor. There was a pause, then the sound of the blind grappling up. A face peered out at them, eyes blinking in the light. Evidently the other had been asleep and the knock had wakened him.

'The last call for breakfast, Monsieur,' called the conductor, bending close to the glass.

The other shook his head emphatically. The cold eyes lifted from the conductor's face and fixed themselves on

Carradine. There was recognition in them and something else that sent a little shiver along his back. How in God's name had the other managed to get on board the train? It was the fat man who had been hounding them all the way across Europe!

A moment later, the blind was pulled down again. The conductor turned. 'Was that your friend?' he asked politely.

Carradine shook his head slowly. There was no expression at all on his face. 'No,' he said quietly. 'I think he must have missed the train. It's of no consequence. No doubt there will be word for me when we reach Paris.'

'I understand, Monsieur.' The conductor gave a brisk nod and walked off along the corridor with the smooth easy gait of one who was used to the swaying train. His shoulders scarcely ever touched the sides of the corridor.

Carradine returned to tell the others.

'Are you sure it's the same man?' For the second time, Francesca asked the question. She bit her lower lip and her fingers twisted a little nervously in her lap. There was a curious expression in her eyes.

'There's no doubt about it. But let's not panic. We expected something like this.'

'It would not have happened if you had done as I asked and taken the plane from Vienna,' she said harshly. 'Now we're caught like flies in a web, not knowing when he means to make his move.' She reached out a hand towards him and then drew it back sharply.

'Do you have any ideas?' asked Ubyenkov.

'I've always thought that the best method of defence was attack,' Carradine said. 'I doubt if he will make any move before it's dark. A lot is going to depend on us getting in our move first.'

'You mean to kill him?' There was a touch of horror in the professor's voice.

'If it's necessary — yes.' There was no emotion in Carradine's tone. He went on dispassionately. 'I can understand how you feel. This is a deadly game that we are playing and when it comes to the showdown, it'll be either him or us. Make no mistake about it. He'll kill us as just as surely as he would swat a fly. All he needs is the opportunity.'

'I see.' The other sat back into his seat, turned his head and stared out of the window. He seemed to have drawn into himself. It was clear that the way in which Carradine was calmly discussing the death, the murder in fact, of another human being had shocked him deeply. Well, thought Carradine tautly, that was just too bad. By now, Ubyenkov should know how these things were. He ought to know, judging by what had happened back there in Balchik. Carradine did not know what had happened to the men who had helped Ubyenkov to escape from Russia and get into Bulgaria, but he could make a good guess.

'You must be careful,' said the girl in a soft voice. 'He is a dangerous man. He will not hesitate to kill you.'

'I don't intend to give him the chance. He knows that we are on the train. He recognised me at once. Fortunately, I feel sure he is alone. Why he's playing a lone hand I don't know. These men usually work in pairs.'

'Perhaps Kreznikov doesn't want to arouse our suspicions.' She seemed to have got over her earlier nervousness.

The train gave a deep, wailing moan and a second later, they thundered into a tunnel. With an effort, Carradine closed his mind to everything but what lay ahead of him. He tried to put himself into the mind of that man in the compartment in the second carriage. When would the other make his move? It was certain that he would not want to arouse any suspicion on the part of the other passengers. The chances were, it would happen after dark and shortly before they arrived at a station where he would be able to leave the train and vanish into the night.

Now that the other knew he had recognised him, he would be doubly cautious. Whenever he opened the door of his compartment to anyone he would have his hand close to the gun he was undoubtedly carrying.

The simple, commonsense answer to

the problem was for Carradine to station himself somewhere where he could watch the other's compartment as soon as it grew dark, and take him by surprise. If the man was travelling alone on the train, then everything should be reasonably uncomplicated. He felt certain that he was as resourceful as the other, that his training had been as thorough as his adversary's, so why panic? The train sped out of the tunnel into the glare of sunlight. Blinking his eyes to adjust them to the brightness, he watched the distant blue sheen of the Adriatic in the distance, a welcome change to the rugged sky-rearing the mountains which had been their lot for most of the journey.

* * *

The touch of Francesca's hand on his arm woke Carradine sometime later. Blinking the sleep from his eyes, he sat upright in his seat and glanced through the window. There were the rich reds and golds of a glorious sunset flaming in the

west. He reckoned they must be somewhere between Vicenza and Verona by
now.

'What time is it?' he asked.

She glanced at her watch. 'Almost nine
o'clock. It will be dark soon.'

He nodded. Taking the small gun from
his pocket, he checked it carefully, aware
that she was watching him closely.

'Are you sure you don't want me to
come with you, Steve?' she asked. There
was a peculiar lilt to her voice as she
spoke. He looked up sharply, slipping the
gun back into his pocket. Good God, he
thought, she actually wants to come along
and make sure he's killed, that this time
he's off our necks for good.

'You're a bloodthirsty little vixen, aren't
you?' he said with a tight smile. Then he
shook his head slowly. 'You'd better
remain here with the professor. Just in
case they do have another man on the
train. Keep your eyes and ears open.'

'I'll be careful,' she said in a low voice.

By the time they left Verona, it was
almost completely dark. The last trace of
colour was fading swiftly from the sky

over the Lombardy plain and the moon was swinging on its back in the west. Carradine waited tensely for another five minutes. There was a lot to be done and he could feel the tightness in his throat, the muscles constricting. There was nothing different to the noises of the train, nothing to indicate that very soon, possibly within the next few minutes, a man was going to die, swiftly and surely. He smiled grimly to himself as he imagined what would happen if the rest of the passengers knew this, the consternation which would be caused, the common feeling of horror. He knew there were still people in the world who looked upon this train as a symbol of adventure and romance; few realised that there were times when that idea was very close to the truth. In the old days, it had been the means of escape for political refugees from Russia and other countries of Eastern Europe. Now there was very little of that going on. But the Orient Express still played an important role in international politics and intrigue. True there was less of it now than before the war.

But there was still some drug smuggling going on from East to West and vice-versa, and it was far easier to use than the planes which now linked the capitals. Circumstances made the customs checks here far less rigorous than at the air terminals.

He got to his feet, looked down at the girl, then stepped over the legs of the sleeping professor and opened the compartment door.

There was a single dim light showing in the corridor, throwing long shadows between the other doors. He held himself straight as he made his way forward, walking on the balls of his feet, feeling the endless sway of the carriage under him.

The blind was still down over the window of the compartment in which the fat man had been. It struck Carradine that perhaps the other was expecting him to do something like this, that the compartment was empty, and the other was somewhere further along the train, hoping to take him by surprise. If that were so, he would have to be doubly careful.

Moving on past the compartment, he came to the end of the carriage and stood there near the door, leaning his shoulders against the wall at his back. From there he could see all the way along the corridor.

He waited patiently. Minutes passed and there was still no movement from the compartment a short distance away. What, if anything, was going on in there behind that blind? he wondered tensely. Was the other simply waiting until he judged the time was right? Would he go creeping silently along the corridor just as he had a few moments ago? The chances were that the man already knew which compartment was theirs. He would go straight to it and use a gun, preferably one fitted with a silencer — or maybe he would wait until they entered the Simplon Tunnel.

The train began to slow. Glancing out of the window, Carradine made out the lights around the curve. This would be Domodossola. There would be no customs check in these carriages which were going through all the way to Paris. They would wait here for perhaps fifteen or twenty minutes and then go on through the Simplon and across Switzerland.

With an effort, he forced his taut muscles to relax. Since the other had not made any move yet, it was unlikely that he would do so until they pulled out of Domodossola.

The train stopped with a clanking of couplings. In the distance, he could hear the opening and shutting doors, the sound of voices. The Italian customs took fifteen minutes. Then the train was off again, the station slid out of sight and Carradine straightened. Why in God's name didn't the other make a move? The girl would be getting worried by now. He hoped that she would do exactly as he had told her and not leave the professor to come looking for him. If she did that and got in the way at the wrong moment it could spoil everything and —

His thoughts stopped. He tensed himself. There was a soft click, barely audible, then the door of the nearby compartment was opening. He saw the widening strip of dark shadow and guessed that the man inside had switched off the light before opening the door.

Pushing himself back out of sight, he waited. The click of the door being closed reached him a few seconds later. Carradine cautiously moved his head to one side, keeping the rest of his body still. The dark, broad shape of the man emerged into sight, his back to Carradine, as he made his way slowly and silently along the corridor. Carradine felt a slight trickle sweat on his forehead and resisted the urge to rub it away.

The train clattered its way over points, jerking abruptly to one side. In front of Carradine, the fat man reached out a hand and grabbed the rail tightly to keep himself upright. Now, thought Carradine. Gripping the gun in his right hand, he tiptoed from his hiding place and padded along the corridor in pursuit.

8

DARK REVELATION

The man had reached the end of the corridor and stood poised near the interconnecting door. He seemed to be listening for something as he stood there, his back to Carradine. For a long moment there was no sound but the intermittent rattle of steel on steel as the wheels rumbled over the points. Then they were on the main line again and the wheels resumed their smooth rhythm. The other moved forward, paused, then began to turn as some animal instinct seemed to warn him of the closeness of danger.

Carradine saw the flabby features turn as the man twisted his blubbery neck around, saw the eyes widen in sudden understanding and realisation. In one violent cork-screwing motion that took Carradine completely by surprise, the other threw himself on the corner of the corridor, his right hand dropping to his pocket. Carradine's muscles uncoiled. The other man then threw himself back at the same moment, his ponderous weight crashing against Carradine's chest as he moved forward. He had anticipated the man's move for the gun in his pocket, but the savage thrust took him off balance. Staggering, he fell back against the window and felt the metal rail hit him hard on the back, across the shoulders.

The man swung with a tightly bunched fist and the blow hit Carradine on the side of the head, sending him sprawling to the floor of the corridor. With a sudden grunt, the other dropped his knees on to Carradine's stomach, his hands groping forward for his throat.

It was impossible in the confined space to twist and throw the man off, just as it was impossible for him to move his arm and drag the gun free. Nails dug into the flesh of his throat as the other began to squeeze, lips drawn back from his teeth. The man hissed something through his parted lips and for a moment, inexplicably, his grip around Carradine's throat loosened as he tried to right himself, his legs hooked on either side of the other's body.

With a superhuman effort, Carradine got his left arm free. He did not waste time or strength in trying to hurl the other off. The corridor was too narrow for him to have any hope of that. Now that the first shock of surprise was over, his mind was working swiftly and smoothly. All of the lessons he had learned in London, lessons that had been taught by a small, wizened Japanese man who looked as though he could not hurt a fly, came back to him. His fingers stiffened, the edge of his palm straight. There was little room in which to move his arm, but enough for his purpose. His hand moved less than six inches but when it connected with the bone just behind his attacker's ears, there was a hollow, crunching thud and the man's head fell back on his rubbery neck. He put up both hands to his throat, gasping horribly for breath, the muscles down the side of his neck completely paralysed by the savage blow. His eyes were wide and staring and all of the life seemed to have gone from his body. Thrusting now with all the strength in his legs, drawing up his knees and twisting them a little to the side, Carradine toppled the other into the more open space immediately in front of the interconnecting door.

For several seconds, Carradine lay on his back, panting hoarsely, sucking air down into his tortured lungs. He stared up at the faint light bulb near the roof of the corridor almost immediately above his head and blinked his eyes several times in an effort to focus properly. Slowly, the roaring in his head went away. Staggering, he managed to get to his feet, holding on to the rail to maintain his balance. There was a shuddering roar, a blast of air passed the outside of the door, and the train thundered into the Simplon Tunnel.

Reeling, he stood over the fallen man. The blow had only partially stunned him and already he was trying to get to his feet. Carradine tugged the gun from his pocket and thumbed forward the safety catch. The sound of a gunshot would not carry far above the ear-splitting roar of the train thrown back from the walls of the tunnel.

'No!' The man on the floor threw up an arm over his face as if to ward off the bullet. At the same time, he kicked out with a foot and caught Carradine on the shin. For a second the agony of the blow, lancing through his leg, made it impossible for him to do anything. Quick to follow up his advantage, the man braced his back against the side of the carriage and lashed out again with his feet. The toecap caught Carradine on the ankle and he felt his leg give under him. His body was flung back against the door. He wondered if his ankle had been broken by the savage force of that blow.

With a violent surge of strength, the other pushed himself to his feet and stood there swaying slightly, his arms hanging loosely by his side, the fingers curled. He had dropped the gun and knew he had no chance of reaching it.

Teeth bared, he moved in. An arm swung, the fist catching Carradine on the face. There was a taste of blood in his mouth and it felt as though his teeth had been smashed through the flesh of his lower lip. Carradine was seized with a surging wave of red-hot anger. He caught the man's arm as it came swinging for him again, gripped the wrist tightly and twisted. The other uttered a bleating yelp of pain and tried to pull himself free. Moving swiftly sideways, Carradine hauled with all of his strength, swinging the man around.

There was a yell, just audible above the sound of the train, a sound that had risen to an abrupt crescendo as the glass of the door splintered under the man's weight. He fell back, overbalanced. Arms and legs flailing for a moment, the other hung there, incredibly, while the blast of air that screamed along the outside of the thundering train caught and tore at his body, dragging him slowly but inexorably through the window. For a second, it was hard for Carradine to believe that it was actually happening. He half-reached out to catch at the other's legs, to drag him back into the train. There was a final shriek as the other suddenly realised what was happening to him and his body slid out of the train and vanished.

The harsh, stinging smell of the air inside the tunnel caught at the back of Carradine's nostrils as he stood there, sucking air down into his heaving lungs. Sweat was cold on his forehead and his shirt was clinging stickily to his back. Slowly, he moved towards the door. Splintered glass crunched under his feet. He stuck his head out and tried to look back along the tunnel, but it was impossible to see anything. The wind caught at his hair, plastering it over his sweating forehead. There was the flash of light on the black walls of the tunnel, but that was all.

Letting his breath go through his parted lips, he pulled his head back, glanced down at his feet and picked up the two guns lying on the floor of the corridor. No one seemed to have heard anything and he knew that if he stayed there, he would have to answer awkward questions, that he would probably be taken off the train at Lausanne and questioned. He would be backed up by London, of course, and strings would be pulled to have him released, with everything carried out discreetly and undramatically. But that would defeat his purpose. His prime objective was to get Professor Ubyenkov to London and nothing was to be allowed to stand in the way of that.

He gave a deep sigh and made his way quickly back along the corridor to the compartment. The girl looked up quickly as he opened the door and went inside. The look on her face changed as she saw the blood on his face.

'You're hurt,' she said concernedly. 'Did you — ?'

'He's dead,' he said tautly. 'He fell out of the train.'

'And when they find that he's vanished?'

Carradine shrugged. He took out his handkerchief and wiped at the blood on his lips. 'There's nothing to connect his disappearance with us. He could have felt ill, gone out into the corridor for some air, opened the window at the end of the carriage and then overbalanced, smashing the glass in the process.'

'Do you honestly think they will come to that conclusion?'

'No, but it's best explanation I can offer at the moment.' He leaned his head back against a seat and fingered the bruises on his throat.

★ ★ ★

They drew into Lausanne a little after three o'clock that morning. Even at that hour, the platform seemed to be crowded with people. Carradine stood at the window, looking up and down the station, but there was no unusual activity to be seen. Either the broken glass of the door had not been noticed yet, which seemed unlikely, or no sinister reason had as yet been attached to it. He forced himself to relax. There was no reason, of course, why anyone should go along that corridor, checking on whether anyone was missing.

They stood for almost half an hour at the platform and then, just when Carradine felt certain that something had been noticed and they were waiting for the police, the train began to move out. The lights of the station slid away into the distance behind them and they were on the last lap of the journey to France.

He dozed on and off during the rest of the night. When dawn came and they passed through Dijon, he stretched himself and stuck his legs out straight in front of him. For the first time since leaving Bulgaria, he had the feeling that they were definitely going to make it. Surely Kreznikov could not touch them now, he thought wearily. Another three hours or so and they would be in Paris. He felt a faint smile come to his lips. He would have to say goodbye to Francesca there, go on to the airport and try to get on the first plane for London. Maybe they would meet again, though under more congenial circumstances, he hoped.

The sun rose, round and red. Slowly, it began to climb up into the cloudless heavens, lost its redness and assumed a fiery glow that flooded the countryside through which they were passing with a rich, warm yellow light. Everything looked different out there, he thought.

More friendly. He recognised several of the landmarks now, and could use them to estimate how far they were from Paris.

The girl woke, rubbed her eyes and looked about her. Carradine leaned over and touched Ubyenkov's knee. The other grunted, then opened his eyes.

'Sorry to wake you so soon,' he said, 'but I thought you might like to see this. We're in France. Another couple of hours and we should be arriving in Paris. Then it's on to London and freedom as far as you're concerned.'

Ubyenkov nodded. He said slowly: 'I wonder why the English will be so glad to see me. Because of myself, or because of the process which I have discovered.'

'That's surely a pessimistic outlook,' Carradine said. 'They may want to deny that it was your process which attracted us to you in the first place, and I very much doubt if my Government or any other for that matter, would spend time and money getting you out of Bulgaria, unless you had something like this to offer.'

'At least, you are very frank,' said

Ubyenkov harshly.

'In my line of business, there is very little time for the niceties of life. I have my orders and it's up to me to see that I carry them out.'

'Of course. But in spite of that, I would like to thank you both for what you have done for me.'

'We aren't safe just yet,' said Francesca sharply. 'Better not count on that until you reach London.'

'She's right,' Carradine cautioned. He touched his lips gingerly where they were slightly swollen. For a moment, he thought about the man who had been following them on the train. Had his body been discovered yet, lying somewhere alongside the gleaming rail inside the Simplon Tunnel? Somehow, it did not seem likely.

★   ★   ★

The Orient Express ran into Paris exactly on time. As he helped the girl down from the train, Carradine looked about him, eyeing the crowd that jostled around

256

them as the rest of the passengers alighted. Curiously, the feeling of danger, which had left him a little just after that man had died on the train, was stronger now. Here they were in a friendly country, away from the Balkan states and yet the feeling was back. He tried to ignore it, the reassuring weight of the gun in his pocket. They walked down the platform, into the station square with the rest of the crowd.

No one seemed to be giving them a second glance and as they stepped out into the street, he told himself that he was merely being foolish, sensing danger where none existed.

He paused at the edge of the pavement and made to lift a hand for a taxi. The girl said quickly: 'I will arrange for you to get to the airport, Steve. It would be far safer if you were to go in one of our cars. It will only take me a few moments to arrange it. They may have someone watching the station just in case. If they had that man on the train to watch for us, you can be sure that they have made further arrangements just in case he did make a mistake.'

Carradine hesitated, then nodded. What she had said was perfectly true. He cursed himself for not considering it. The fact that they had reached Paris had overridden his natural caution. Compared with Bulgaria and Hungary, the French capital seemed so close to London that he had overlooked the fact that the tentacles of the Russian Secret Service reached out all the way across Europe and those who directed it seldom did anything without having a second string to their bow. Men were fallible and they were the first to realise it. What did it matter to them if one other man was killed and his body vanished off the Orient Express just so long as they had someone else keeping an eye on things further along line. They wouldn't give up until he ushered Ubyenkov into the Chief's office at Headquarters.

He waited with Ubyenkov while the girl went over to one of the telephones. Through the glass door he could see her dialling a number. Two minutes later, she came out and walked over to them, smiling.

'They will have a car here shortly,' she told him. 'It will take us to the airport.'

Exactly five minutes later a black limousine turned up, stopping smoothly by the kerb in front of them. The man behind the wheel was a typical French chauffeur. He got out and opened the door for them, then slipped in behind the wheel once more. The girl sat beside him in the front. Without a word being spoken their car moved off, into the stream of traffic.

'I'll say this for the Deuxieme Bureau,' Carradine said quietly, sitting back. 'They certainly are efficient.'

The girl smiled, but said nothing. The chauffeur drove the big car with a calm and relaxed assurance, a quiet efficiency that seemed to be the hallmark of the Deuxieme Bureau.

Leaving the centre of the city behind, they took one of the wide avenues out to the outskirts, past the little wayside cafés with their multi-coloured awnings, which seemed such a part of Parisian life. If only it were possible to stay here for a few days, he thought, to relax utterly and

259

completely after the nightmare of the past three days and nights. But that was utterly out of the question.

They turned off into a narrow street where there was very little traffic. Carradine sat back for a moment, then jerked himself upright in his seat. 'This isn't the way out to the airport,' he said sharply. 'We should have — '

'Of course not.' The girl had turned her head to look at him. She was still smiling, but there was something in that smile which froze Carradine's thoughts.

'What do you think you're doing, Francesca?' he said harshly. 'If this is your idea of a joke — If you think you can take the professor to the Deuxieme Bureau to question him first, then I'd advise you to think again. It only needs a word from me to the Head of the Bureau and — '

Francesca shook her head slowly. The sunlight, streaming in through the window, caught the yellow hair, sending warm gleams of gold through it. 'You don't understand, Steve, even yet,' she murmured softly.

He felt a little warning tingle along his spine, and reached down with his hand towards the gun still resting snugly in his pocket. The one that he had taken from the fat man on the train was in his case. What was it in the girl's voice that heightened the feeling of danger in his mind? The crisp note of authority, or sheer confidence?

Her hand moved and came into sight above the top of the front seat as she twisted round a little more. The gun in her hand did not waver as the barrel lined itself up to his chest. 'I think this will save any further argument,' she said coldly. 'You know, you were quite correct when you said that we have agents watching everywhere, even as far west as Paris.'

Carradine felt his mouth go dry and swallowed thickly. So it had been a trap all along and he had fallen into it with his eyes wide open. He thought once again of that man he had killed on the train. Almost as if she divined his thoughts the girl said:

'You were supposed to think that I was on your side. Even in Tamariu, I had been ordered to keep an eye on you, to learn everything I could about you. And as for that man who was following me, the man you so kindly disposed of on the train. He was working for the Deuxieme Bureau. It was very good of you to get him off my back. I had thought that I might have to do it myself.'

'I think I'm beginning to get the picture now,' said Carradine tautly. 'You can spare me the details.' He felt a sense of disgust run through his mind. How could he have been so criminally blind? Several little points that had been puzzling him began to slot into place and made sense now. Those conversations which she had had with the frontier guards in Bulgaria and Hungary. No wonder she had been able to persuade them to let them through without any questions. She had merely told them who she really was, that she was working for the Russian Secret Service, and they had gone out of their way to speed them across Europe.

He felt a wave of anger go through him. How conveniently, too, had she come on the scene when he had escaped with Ubyenkov from that castle overlooking the Black Sea. She must have been given orders to stick around Balchik just in case something did go wrong and he managed to get away from Kreznikov and his hatchet men.

Hell, what a fool he had been. If only he had paused to think these things out carefully and objectively, he would have seen through this little scheme long before now and he would not have been in the mess he was at this very moment. Here in Paris, so close to England, and his chances of ever seeing London again had receded almost to vanishing point. With an effort, he forced the anger and despair out of his mind. Whatever else happened, he must play along with these two and try to get them off balance. There had to be a way before it was too late.

'Just what is your job?' he asked quietly.

Francesca shrugged her shoulders, not once taking her eyes off his face. 'Let's say that I act as a decoy for Western agents,' she said, a mocking tone to her voice. 'You never really learn, do you? You seem to think that we are nothing more than a lot of foolish people, used only to the ways of violence, with no subtlety about us at all. It's this continual underestimation of us which will eventually lead to your downfall.'

'You really believe that, don't you?' he said, his tone deliberately scornful. 'You have such a high opinion of yourselves that you fail to recognise your own weaknesses.'

'What do you mean by that?' she asked sharply.

Carradine gave a faint grin. He had touched a nerve, he felt sure of that, by even suggesting that she might have overlooked some vital point.

'You're in Paris now,' he said quietly. He forced evenness into his voice, knowing just how precarious his own position was. He had to make the girl believe that he had more behind him than he really had. Whether or not he could pull it off, he did not know. But he had to try his damnedest, because it was the only chance he had. He knew without question that if he tried to go for the gun in his pocket, or for that which the girl held so steadily in her hand, she would shoot him without a second thought. She had been trained to kill just as he had, and she would not hesitate to do so. He remembered that unholy look in her eyes when he had walked out of that compartment on the Orient Express, going out to kill that fat man who had been following them. The same bright stare was in her eyes now.

'And why should you think that being in Paris worries us?' Her voice was sarcastic. 'If you're relying on the Deuxieme Bureau to help you out of this mess, then you're wasting your time. You will quietly disappear and our mutual friend, the professor, will be on his way to Moscow by tonight. You upset my plans by insisting that we travel on the Orient Express. Everything was ready for us at Vienna. That had to be cancelled, of course. But it mattered little in the end.' Her smile widened a little, showing the even white teeth. 'I must admit now though, that when you warned me that man from the Deuxieme Bureau was on the train, I was worried. If he had managed to get to you before you killed him, he might have told you everything and there was just a chance you would have believed him.'

She nodded towards the gun in her hand, then let her glance flicker momentarily towards Ubyenkov. 'You didn't know that I had this gun with me. If you had come back with that man I would have shot the professor.' Cautiously, she went on: 'You don't know how close to death you were then, Professor Ubyenkov.'

'And now?' Carradine said very softly. 'What do you intend to do now?'

'We have a place on the outskirts of Paris where you will be quite safe until dark. Then you will be taken to the Seine. By the time your body is washed up, we shall be back in Russia and this rather unpleasant chapter will have been closed.'

'I see.' He rubbed his mouth and saw the gun lift a fraction as the girl followed the move. Her knuckles were white as she tightened her finger on the trigger. 'Be very careful,' she warned. 'I don't want to have to shoot you here, but if you make

266

any move that I don't like, I will.'

Yes, thought Carradine, you would. How could he have been so mistaken about this girl? He glanced through the window of the car. They were slowing now, moving through one of the slum districts of Paris. Long warehouses lay along either side of the dingy streets, doors hanging lopsidedly on twisted hinges. The river probably lay on the other side of them, he reflected. This was a section of the city he did not know.

They turned a corner. The car stopped a short distance around it. In front of them the road narrowed sharply. Garbage lay in piles down either side of it and a couple of mangy cats ran swiftly away from the car, clambering out of sight of the broken stone wall to one side.

'All right,' snapped the girl. She waved the gun negligently. 'Outside, both of you. And I ought to warn you that Boris here has some very special methods of dealing with anyone who doesn't do exactly as he is told.'

'So I can imagine,' murmured Carradine through his teeth. He thrust his legs out of the car and stood up. The smell of the river was in his nostrils now and he knew he had been right about it being close by.

'Stand there for a moment,' ordered the girl sharply as he made to move forward, 'and place your hands behind your neck.'

Carradine did as he was told. The chauffeur padded up behind him, ran his hand expertly over his body, located the gun the girl had given him and took it from his pocket.

'You're both taking a bit of a gamble, aren't you?' Carradine said. 'Suppose that the Deuxieme Bureau have someone watching the station for the Orient Express. They could have followed us here.'

The girl shook her head. The possibility did not seem to worry her. She said patiently, as explaining things to a little child: 'There was no one to let them know you were on the train, I'm afraid. If you want my opinion, I would say they still believe we are somewhere in Austria or Yugoslavia. They won't get around to worrying about us until it's far too late.

Now follow Boris and keep your hands were I can see them.'

The chauffeur led the way up a rickety wooden stairway, into the top floor of one of the long buildings. As he went inside, into the dark, cool shadows of the place, Carradine looked about him carefully, taking in every detail, filing it away in his mind. He did not know what was important and what was not, but if they were to have any chance of getting out of this mess alive, then he could afford to overlook nothing.

Boxes lined one wall of the long room, reaching all the way to the ceiling. There was plenty of open space on one side, the side facing the alley. Light came from four skylights, set at regular intervals in the sloping ceiling. There was the musty smell of a long abandoned place in his nostrils, of dust that had lain on the floor, undisturbed, for a long time.

'I suppose that we make ourselves comfortable while we wait,' he said quietly.

Francesca motioned to the packing cases. 'I'm afraid that here we are not

269

exactly used to luxury. But if you get to make yourself comfortable, you have only a few hours to wait. It may, of course, interest you to know that your demise has been carefully planned down to the last detail.'

'The thoroughness of the Russian Secret Service,' he said.

'Exactly.'

The chauffeur moved over to the door and stood there with his shoulders leaning against the wooden upright. He took out a cigarette, and lit it and stood quite relaxed, smoking. But his eyes never strayed for very long from Carradine and Ubyenkov, who sat slumped on one of the cases, his shoulders hunched forward. Carradine eyed Ubyenkov out of the corner of his eye, wondering whether the other would back him up if he made any move. Somehow, he doubted it. The other had seemed broken, as if he had already resigned himself to being taken back to Russia. God alone knew what would happen to the poor bastard when they got him there, he thought grimly. The tales told about the salt mines in Siberia were undoubtedly exaggerated, but they still existed and if he wasn't executed for a crime against the state, or put in prison for the rest of his life, then that was where they might send him. Ubyenkov would pay dearly for his attempt to escape from Russia.

Carefully, he measured the distance to the chauffeur at the door. Too far for him to hope to reach the other before the man killed him. The girl would be easier. She was standing less than a couple of feet away, watching him out of coldly amused eyes. Use her as a shield? It was a possibility, but even that might not work. He hadn't any guarantee that the chauffeur would not shoot her just to make sure that he and Ubyenkov did not escape. The girl herself had said that it mattered little if they lost a man, many men, so long as they carried out their assignment.

There was the muffled hoot of a boat on the river nearby. The rattle of a tram in the distance sounded. The everyday sounds of Paris, he thought vaguely. The girl took a quick glance at her wristwatch.

'Worried that someone might happen along and see the car?' he said softly. 'If they do, they might start asking questions, may even come along looking for the owner and — '

'Shut up!' snapped the girl sharply. 'Another interruption from you and I shall kill you here and now. There is very little point in keeping you alive. Come to think of it, that might be the best thing to do. No doubt your mind is working overtime trying to think of some way out of this, of turning the tables on us.'

'The idea had occurred to me,' he said quietly. He felt tense, but tried not to show it in his voice. Inwardly, he was thinking, what a bloody stupid way for him to die. Here in this dusty, abandoned warehouse on the outskirts of Paris, with everyone in London no doubt thinking he was still somewhere in Eastern Europe, not worrying unduly about him or Ubyenkov. By the time they got around to worrying, it would be too late. He would be dead and Ubyenkov would be beyond the Iron Curtain, out of reach of anyone from the West.

272

The chauffeur pushed himself away from the doorway, tossed a cigarette butt down into the alley below and moved nearer. Carradine felt the muscles of his chest tighten. If only he could entice the other closer to him and get both him and the girl within range of that lighter of his. He was suddenly very glad that he had not fully explained this to the girl. He had been on the point of doing so when they had met in Balchik.

Getting to his feet, he stretched himself, yawning. The girl stiffened and pulled up the barrel of the gun.

He slipped his hand into his pocket, pulled out the cigarette case and extracted a cigarette, thrusting it between his lips, glad to notice his fingers were stone steady. The chauffeur had moved towards him, eyes alert. Now he was less than six feet away, a tall, looming shadow in the grey dimness.

Carradine lit the cigarette and blew smoke into the air. He held the lighter loosely in his hand. 'You know, Francesca,' he said very softly, 'you made one big mistake that gave you away long before we reached

Paris. A mistake that is going to prove to be your undoing.'

'Oh?' The girl's voice sounded bored. 'May I ask what it was? Perhaps the next time I will be able to ensure that it doesn't happen again.'

'You made it so obvious that the man who was following us had to be killed once we discovered he was on the train. I suppose it was because he was the one person who could spoil everything for you.' He smiled. 'And you also forgot that I had a chance to talk with the conductor. How do you know I didn't ask him to send a message through to the Headquarters of the Deuxieme Bureau in Paris, asking for them to keep a watch on the station, to follow us?'

For a second, there was a look of alarm in the girl's eyes, then she shook her head. 'No, you didn't do that,' she said. 'Besides, even if you did it would make no difference now. The minute there is any sound outside, you both die. By the time anyone gets here, Boris and I will be gone and — '

Carefully, turning the lighter slightly in

his fingers, Carradine pressed down on it with his thumb, keeping it there. The chauffeur uttered a sharp cry of pain and staggered back as the liquid struck him, vaporising instantly on his skin. The gun in the girl's hand went off with a loud roar and Carradine felt a red-hot poker lay a searing finger along his arm. Then the potent chemical had struck her and the gun dropped from her fingers as she reeled back, falling over the body of the chauffeur.

Bending swiftly, he took the gun from beneath the girl's body and straightened up, holding his breath so as not to inhale more of the fumes than was necessary. He stepped back quickly. Tears half-blinded him and there was a stabbing pain in his chest, a tightness. Turning, he grabbed Ubyenkov by an arm and dragged him to the door.

He sucked the clean, pure air down into his lungs and felt the pounding ache in his head fade perceptibly. God, but that stuff was potent. Just a few whiffs and he had almost been out.

A quarter of an hour later, he was

seated in the Headquarters of the Deuxieme Bureau in the heart of Paris. Francesca and Boris were safely tucked away in one of the other rooms in the building where they would be interrogated once they recovered from the effects of the tear gas.

'I have sent word to London,' said the tall man behind the desk softly. 'They will send a special plane to meet you at Orly in an hour. Two hours from now, and you should both be back in London.' He smiled. 'I suppose I am right in saying that you will be glad to see the last of Europe for a little while?'

Carradine nodded, drank down the last of the whisky, and set the empty glass down on the desk in front of him. He felt wonderful now, far better than at any time since he had left London.

'And those two?' he asked, making a gesture to the other room.

The man waved a negligent hand. 'You do not have to worry about them, *mon ami*. I shall personally see that everything is taken care of. They will tell us all that we want to know of their organisation.

When they are of no further use to us, then . . . ' He deliberately left the remainder of his sentence unsaid, but Carradine could guess at it. He felt a stab of regret. She was a very beautiful girl. If only things could have been different, if only they had not been working on opposite sides, if only . . .

But there were too many 'ifs' in the world for him to worry about this one. He tried to tell himself that the girl must have known what the consequences of failure were, whether from her own people, or those of the West. This was the cold war and there were casualties in it just as there had been in the hot one. He rubbed his chin, feeling the beard under his fingers. He needed a bath and a shave before he went back to London to report.

THE END

SHERLOCK HOLMES TAKES A HAND

Vernon Mealor

An exciting trio of tales following the escapades of Colonel Sebastian Moran, 'one of the best shots in the world' and the 'second most dangerous man in London', according to Sherlock Holmes. Find out how Moran achieves his position at the right hand of Professor Moriarty in 'The Hurlstone Selection'; shares lodgings with Holmes, Watson, and Mrs Hudson in 'The Man with the Square-Toed Boots'; and turns his skills to art theft in 'The Disappearance of Lord Lexingham'.

THE THIRD KEY

Gerald Verner

The Reverend Colin Armitage receives a parcel one morning containing a key and the intriguing message: 'This is Bluebeard's first key.' The key belongs to the cottage of a woman named Sylvia Shand, who is found there, strangled. A few days later, Bluebeard's second key arrives by post and the district nurse is found strangled in similar circumstances. The police believe a homicidal maniac is loose in the village but Armitage has other ideas. And then a third key arrives . . .

MORE CASES OF A PRIVATE EYE

Ernest Dudley

This second book of Ernest Dudley's stories about his London-based private eye character, Nat Craig, finds Craig's clients making up a pretty varied collection. Young, wealthy women getting themselves blackmailed; wealthier men or women who have the jitters over the safety of their precious family heirlooms; occasionally even members of the ex-crook class, appeal to him for help. And not infrequently Craig finds himself confronted with grisly murders, testing his tough resourcefulness and considerable powers of deduction.

Classic British crime stories with an intriguing psychological slant on characters from every walk of life!

A CANDIDATE FOR CONSPIRACY

Steve Hayes

Yesterday he was a spy. Today he's a Washington politician. Tomorrow he could be the next President of the United States. Soon he could be in control of one of the world's most powerful nations — unless a daredevil adventurer and his beautiful accomplice can stop him. But that's a big if . . .